MW00437930

Red Havoc Bad Bear

(Red Havoc Panthers, Book 5)

T. S. JOYCE

Red Havoc Bad Bear

ISBN-13: 978-1548377434
ISBN-10: 1548377430
Copyright © 2017, T. S. Joyce
First electronic publication: June 2017

T. S. Joyce
www. tsjoyce.com

NOTE FROM THE AUTHOR:

This book is a work of fiction. The names, characters, places, and incidents are products of the writer's imagination or have been used fictitiously and are not to be construed as real. Any resemblance to persons, living or dead, actual events, locale or organizations is entirely coincidental. The author does not have any control over and does not assume any responsibility for third-party websites or their content.

Published in the United States of America

First digital publication: June 2017
First print publication: June 2017

Editing: Corinne DeMaagd
Cover Photography: Wander Aguiar
Cover Model: Jonny James

DEDICATION

For the other half of Team Havok.

I got really lucky the day you decided to be my friend.

- bt

ACKNOWLEDGMENTS

I couldn't write these books without some amazing people behind me. A huge thanks to Corinne DeMaagd, for helping me to polish my books, and for being an amazing and supportive friend. Looking back on our journey here, it makes me smile so big. You are an incredible teammate, C!

To Jonny James, the model for this cover—he is a truly good man and a hard worker. Thank you for keeping me steady behind the scenes with your friendship and unending support. And also...for always sticking up for me. That's a big deal.

Thanks to Wander Aguiar and his amazing team for this shot for the cover. It was a custom shoot and I was so happy with it the first time I saw the picture. You always come through in big ways for me.

And last but never least, thank you, awesome reader. You have done more for me and my stories than I can even explain on this teeny page. You found my books, and ran with them, and every share, review, and comment makes release days so incredibly special to me.

1010 is magic and so are you.

ONE

War had never been hard for Jathan Barns to watch before.

It was part of life for a shifter, especially a Gray Back. His crew, like all the crews in Damon's Mountains, were no strangers to fighting. Wars were fought under human radar, quietly, quickly, to inflict maximum damage to those who would come after his people, but minimal damage to the shifter reputation in the public eye.

No...war had never been hard to watch...until now.

3

He knelt on the pine needle-covered forest floor between two oaks and, in agitation, scratched his beard with his thumbnail. Lynn was at it again. Over and over, she'd called the shifters here to war, one at a time. Jathan had watched her from a distance over the last three weeks, and he wasn't the only one. Creed Barnett, alpha of the Gray Backs, stood a hundred yards off, watching Lynn's panther battle a monster she'd pulled from the mountains. Crazy Lynn had called Nox, the son of the Cursed Bear, to fight her. Clearly, she had a death wish. From the pissed-off look in Creed's dark eyes, he knew it too. She was trying to end it. Again.

Jathan lifted his phone and took a picture. He'd done it every time she'd called a shifter to fight. He didn't know why. Maybe soon he would show her the pictures and explain the damage she was really doing to herself. He wanted to throttle her. He wanted to shame her for being weak. Weak, weak, weak. Eden, Lynn's best friend and Red Havoc crewmate, had told Jathan it was a broken mating bond that made her snap, but that was bullshit. Mating bonds didn't exist, and love was a crock of crap people pretended to feel so that their lives could have meaning in the short time they were on this earth.

Lynn had snapped because she quit trying.

Jathan spat on the ground as the screaming panther and blond grizzly bear waged a war that had felled two damn trees already with the violence. Jathan knew what was coming. So did Creed. Lynn had a move at the end of a fight when she was getting tired.

Jathan narrowed his eyes at Lynn as she spun and raked her claws against Nox's neck. She was goading him. Pissing him off. Hurting him so he only saw red. She'd been working her way through each member of each crew systematically, looking for one who would lose control. Well, she fucking found it with Nox. He was almost as crazy as her.

Creed was taking his shirt off now, preparing

to Change to stop Nox from what Lynn was begging him to do, but there was no point. A massive silver bruin meandered out of the woods and paced along the edge of the battle. Nox was distracted now. Even if he was crazy, nobody wanted a fight with Beaston.

Lynn had her back to the silver bear, so she didn't know Beaston stalked the fight. She latched onto Nox's throat until the blond bear bellowed in pain, and then she did it. She went weak. She slid to the ground and exposed her neck and asked for a kill bite.

Beaston charged, and Nox backed off. Lynn...weak, broken Lynn, lay there in the dirt, chest heaving, eyes vacant—she'd left this world again. Jathan wanted to yank her up by the scruff of the neck and scream in her face, "Fucking try. Try! Do better than this." He'd wasted his concern for three damn weeks though, and she was no better than when her crew sent her to Creed to try to save her.

"Fuck," Creed muttered. His eyes were too

light to be human, and his face was contorted with rage. He was an alpha who took in the troubled souls and tried to rehab them, but Lynn was too far gone. Creed spun on his heel and disappeared into the woods. Beaston and Nox went their separate ways, while Lynn lay limp, breath steadying out as her long, black tail twitched every three seconds. One, two, three, twitch. One, two, three, twitch.

With an irritated sigh, Jathan stood and made his way to her. When he glared down at the massive, solid black panther, she locked those dead eyes on him. He wanted badly to hate her, so why the fuck was he here? Why did he follow her around, watch every fight, and make a list of the shifters in Damon's Mountains she had called out? Why did he take pictures of her brawling? Why did he so badly dread his own fight with her? She would call him to battle, and he'd never shied away from a fight. He reveled in them. Fighting made him feel steadier. But the thought of fighting Lynn? It made him want to retch for reasons he didn't understand.

It was probably because her Red Havoc Crew kept calling him, and he felt some sense of responsibility for her. Yeah. That was all. Tonight, when she was all tucked up in her little Crazy Lynn treehouse behind the Grayland Mobile Park, he would ride his Harley into town, drink until the whiskey pushed these inconvenient thoughts about a broken girl out of his mind, and he would find a local chick to hook up with. He would come back all better in the morning. Back to his self. Back to the Bad Bear that everyone said he was.

But for now, like after every fight, he picked up her limp body and cradled the giant-ass panther to his chest. He ignored the growling because she never clawed at him, or bit him. She lashed out at everyone else, but not him. Not the person she should be clawing the most. Because a long, long time ago, before she got weak and pitiful, back when she lived just outside of these mountains, she was a tough girl. She'd had a quiet strength when they were kids. He'd watched her in school when she wasn't looking. He'd wanted to figure her out, without getting too close to her, because she'd felt dangerous. But it was him who had been dangerous to her. He'd been to a hundred parties, but they were all a blur in his memory. All but one—the party he'd hurt Lynn at.

The beginning of her end had all started with Jathan.

Her life would probably end because of him, too.

War had never been hard for Jathan Barns to watch before.

Not until the war lived inside of someone he wanted to save.

TWO

Every day was the same as the last. Lynn Matheson winced when Jaxon set her down where he always did—in a yard of dandelions.

Jaxon. Jaxon? She looked around, but this wasn't Red Havoc Territory. Jaxon Barns was up in the Appalachian Mountains with his mate. With Lynn's crew. This wasn't Jaxon, and she wasn't in Red Havoc Woods. This was...what was his name? Identical twin. Funny. Bad. He'd always been in trouble when they were growing up. The local cops knew him by name. He rode a Harley and got arrested and got tattoos and piercings and didn't give a fuck about anything. Bad grizzly, Bad Bear. Jason…no…Jathan. Jathan Barns.

She couldn't muster the energy to hiss as he backed away and sat on the bottom stair of her treehouse. Beaston had built it long ago, and now this was her home for six more days. She was counting down.

Jathan was a hot boy name.

This place didn't even smell like Red Havoc territory. It was all wintergreen and pine sap and oil from the logging equipment up the road.

A hot boy name for a hot boy. He'd always looked good. Time had treated him well. He wasn't lanky anymore. He was built like a tank. A sexy, tatted-up tank.

Her focus was scattering like ashes on the wind.

Where was she again?

She blinked. Time must have disappeared on her. That happened a lot. She came to with a feeling like time had passed, but she had no idea how much. Jathan was still here, but he was leaning back against the stairs, hands behind his head, staring up at the blue sky. It was too damn bright out here, and her body hurt. She wasn't healing very fast anymore. Nox hadn't been a careful fighter. She'd almost had him. So close, if only Beaston had stayed away. Why was everyone here protecting her? Couldn't they see she was already gone? Couldn't they see she was unredeemable? This was Eden's fault. And Jaxon's. And all of Red Havoc who voted she come to the Gray Backs so the alpha could try to save her. She was too far gone for even Creed, though. Everyone here said that, and they were right.

Another blink. More time lost.

The shadow of the tree house was creeping closer across the dandelions. It would reach her soon. Maybe she would feel it, the instant the edge of the shadow touched her. Maybe it would be cold. She hoped she could feel it. It would be nice to feel something before the end.

Jathan was waiting for her to Change back. It was rude to keep him from his life. He always did this—waited for her to tuck her psychotic animal away. She would go through the pain of the Change, and he wouldn't say a word. He would just lift her body up like she was helpless and carry her up the stairs, set her in bed, and leave until tomorrow.

Jathan Barns smelled sick, too. Not as sick as her, but his head was messed up, and that damage made his bear a beast, just like his identical twin brother, Jaxon. Jaxon. Was this Jathan or Jaxon? They looked the same. Same dark brown eyes and black hair. Same massive stature and thick arms and neck. Same smile for everyone but her. He only looked at her in pity or anger, but the fury part she didn't understand. She hadn't asked him to carry her around. What right did he have to be angry?

Six more days, and he would be free from whatever obligation he felt toward her.

With a groan, she forced the Change. It was a

slow process because she did this too much, too often. Her panther didn't let her keep her skin for long. She was sad and angry, just like Lynn, and somewhere along the way, they'd split completely. She was animal and human, shoved in the same body, and both of them hated each other. Neither one of them had been successful at digging out of the hole they'd gotten themselves into. Not even a little.

Jathan narrowed his eyes at her. Pretty brown, and they turned bright green when he was worked up. She used to have a crush on him when they were kids, but he never gave her the time of day. He was too cool for a shy orphan shifter trying to make her foster parents love her enough to keep her. He was a party boy, but she had real-life problems, and even if they lived in the same mountains, they were from two different worlds.

Her voice came out raspy when she asked, "What's your favorite food, Jaxon?"

His eyes tightened at the corners, and his

14

dark eyebrows drew down. "She talks. She talks, but she calls me by my brother's name."

"Jathan, Jathan, Jathan," she whispered three times so she could remember it. She wouldn't, though. Her mind didn't work very well anymore.

"Pizza." He rocked up to the sitting position and cracked his knuckles. "You?"

"I'm Lynn."

"I know your name. I'm asking what is your favorite food."

"Oh. Food. Food is good. I'm hungry."

"What for?"

"Ribs before I hated Red Havoc." Barret had made her ribs to try to draw her out of her treehouse and back into the crew. She wasn't dumb, just broken. She didn't like being manipulated with her favorite things.

"Well, that was a weird fucking answer."

"Chicken fried steak. With gravy."

Lynn pushed herself up on her hands and knees, then settled onto her bent legs. Jathan was staring at her tits now, but she didn't care. Nudity was natural, and all shifters had to deal with it since they were young. Tits were tits. No one had enjoyed the sight of hers since…Brody.

Blink. Time was lost.

When she opened her eyes, she was in the tree house, lying in her bed on top of the covers. And she wasn't even naked anymore. When Lynn sat up, she let out a tiny gasp for the ache in her muscles. She fingered the hem of the sundress Eden had packed for her before she had left Red Havoc Territory. It was white with pink flowers and was, literally, the girliest thing she owned.

The smell of fur hit her nose, and she jerked her attention to the back wall of the treehouse where Jathan stood with his broad back to her, hands clasped behind him as he stared at the marks she'd etched into the wall.

"What the fuck is this?" he asked, his voice low and growly.

"You don't scare me," she murmured. "Nothing does."

He slid her a bright green-eyed glare over his shoulder.

Okay, he was a little scary. Like...fourteen percent intimidating when his scary-beary was at the surface. "What are the marks, Lynn?"

She crossed her arms over her chest. "My countdown. Six more days, and Creed's time is up."

"You mean six more days, and *your* time is up," he snarled. "Put your shoes on."

"What? No. I'm staying here, and you had no right to dress me in this—"

"I'm taking you into town, we're going to eat chicken fried steak, and you're going to actually live for the last six fucking days of your countdown. And I swear to God, if you fight me on a single thing, I'll strap you into my truck and take you so fucking far away from anyone who would put you down, you couldn't scream loud enough to get attention. And I'd make you live out your entire life with me staring at you and counting your billion remaining breaths. Put your fucking shoes on."

Lynn pursed her lips. Okay then.

She slid off the bed, dared to cast him a dirty look, then slipped her feet into a pair of tattered, black flip-flops that didn't match just to spite the bully currently standing against the wall, watching her. He had the same color eyes as Beaston. The snarl in his throat and the weight of his dominance made the air feel like clay in her lungs. Someday, she had no doubt he would be alpha of the Gray Backs. Creed's days were numbered as king of Grayland Mobile Park unless he pushed this bruin out of his territory.

Jathan jerked his chin toward the small bathroom. "Go brush your hair."

"Fuck you."

Jathan was to her so fast he was a blur. He gripped her arm and pulled her into the bathroom, pushed her down onto the closed toilet lid by the shoulder, yanked the brush off the counter, and then he did something that stunned her to her bones. He gentled his hand

and ran the brush through the ends of her snarled, red tresses, then worked his way up.

"You've brushed hair before."

He was quiet so long she thought he would ignore her the rest of the time he forced her to get presentable, but after a while he said in a softer voice, "Willa is my mom. She made me and my brother do this shit for her when she was feeling lazy or had two glasses of wine in her hands and needed help. She's ridiculous."

"You love her."

He huffed a breath. "She's one of the very few things I love. Do you want to do your make-up, or do you want me to? I'm pretty good at making people look like hookers. Mom made me watch stupid fucking tutorials online on how to do smoky eyes, but mostly I will make you look like a frightened raccoon."

Lynn huffed a strange sound, but it startled her, and she jumped. When she looked up at Jathan, he was frowning down at her, but his expression wasn't harsh anymore. It was curious.

"Did you just laugh?"

Blink. Time was lost.

****

Jathan lined her lips with a petal-pink color she kept with her other make-up. God, she was pretty. Always had been. Full lips led to a perfect, little pixie nose, high cheekbones, soft brown eyes slightly slanted like cat eyes, fair skin, a light dusting of freckles he hadn't bothered to hide with foundation because he liked her spots. And that hair—red as fire and flowing down her shoulders in soft, rolling waves. She was too thin now, and her eyes had dark circles under them. They looked vacant, as if she was dead already, especially when she was checked out and staring straight ahead, like right now. But even as a broken bird, she was a swan.

What was he doing?

Squatting down in front of her, he rested his hands on her knees for balance. She was warm and alive, and in six days she wouldn't be anymore. He wanted to puke. Such a waste.

There was a tiny green pot with a Venus Flytrap on the bathroom sink. Someone had hand-painted a name in pink letters. Medusa. It was a healthy, ugly little thing, nice and green with several heads, open, teeth out, waiting for a fly to land and feed it. Medusa. Lynn had a disconnect problem with people. He'd been watching and could see it plain as day, but she had some kind of attachment to this little plant.

How did he know? Because when he'd taken her back to Damon's Mountains from the Red Havoc Territory, she'd cradled the little plant in her lap the entire way to the airport and on the flight to Damon's Mountains. She hadn't said a word to him, and she'd been lost in her head for most of the trip, but she'd uttered three soft-spoken words to Medusa when she thought he wasn't listening. "It'll be okay."

Just to experiment, he cupped Lynn's cheeks. Skin so soft against the callouses of his hands made rough from the logging work he did. "Lynn, can you hear me?"

Nothing. Pupils constricted to pinpoints, her eyes stared straight ahead, looking right through him.

Jathan chewed the corner of his lip a few times and tried again. "Medusa."

Lynn blinked and turned her face slightly. Pupils dilating, she focused on his face. "W-what?" Her lips were pretty as she formed the question.

"Do you want to bring Medusa tonight?" he asked.

"Bring her where?" Her voice was sing-songy and not quite right.

"I'm going to take you out."

Her delicate, ruddy eyebrows drew down in the cutest fucking frown he'd ever seen. "Like on a date?"

Jathan laughed. "Woman, I don't date. I fuck. You don't want a date with me."

Hurt slashed through her eyes for just an instant and confused the shit out of him. "Oh. Then no, I don't need Medusa. She is safe here."

Hmm.

"Do you *want* to call it a date? We can. You only have six days left. Six days, six dates with the Bad Bear. I'll find us lots of trouble. Sound fun?"

The corner of her lip ticked up, then fell. "You think trouble is fun. Trouble isn't fun. Trouble ruins everything."

"Nah, you just found the wrong kind of trouble, little nut." He made a knocking sound while gently rapping his knuckles against the side of her head. What the fuck was he doing? He didn't do rapport with girls. He had this with Mom and Dad and Jaxon, and that was it. Girls were dangerous. This one was the biggest danger of all. She was already half gone.

"I think I'm more than a little nut," she said, her cheeks flushing a pretty pink color. "I'm a big nut. I think I'm crazy. Everyone in Red Havoc calls me Crazy Lynn."

"So does everyone here." Honesty was best. She knew what was happening.

"Do you call me Crazy Lynn?"

Jathan dipped his chin once. "In my head, I do."

More hurt slashed through her eyes, and what the fuck was happening? Broken little kitty. She wasn't the same panther goddess who had left these mountains ten years ago. That Lynn had been destroyed by whatever had happened to her. Now she got hurt by everything. He was the worst one to be taking this on because he wasn't kind, sensitive, or understanding. Likely, he would break her faster.

The world was black and white to him. You fight or you didn't fight, and Lynn wasn't a fighter anymore—but he was. They were too different, and he didn't understand her. And now he'd offered six dates in six days but with the worst intentions. It wasn't to fall for her, or to get her to fall for him. He didn't feel emotion like that, and love was a crock of shit. He was going to manipulate her into living because everything else had failed. And admittedly? He didn't carry a single ounce of guilt for what he was about to do.

"I want to show you something before I take you into town for our first date."

"I don't want dates. Dates lead to dying inside."

Jathan offered her an empty smile. "Well, lucky for you, we're both dead inside already. You call it what you want, and I'll call them dates."

Her cute little frown got deeper before she formed an *O* with her mouth, but she didn't argue. Instead, she pursed her lips and clasped her hands in her lap. "If you're going to show me your dick, I've already seen it."

Jathan bellowed a single, surprised laugh. "You have?"

Lynn nodded. "I watch you Change at night when you think no one can see your monster. I have a monster, too. Soon we'll fight. Clash of the monsters."

Her eyes were going hazy, so Jathan pulled her off the toilet lid quick and turned her around in the mirror so she could see her make-up. He wanted to laugh at the difference between them. He was a foot taller than her, covered in tattoos up to his neck, and his eyes were glowing bright green. While Lynn was a dainty little redhead who looked tiny in front of him and shocked to see her reflection. He would fucking wreck her in the bedroom. Jathan frowned. If that were an option. Which is wasn't, because she was broken and didn't need any wrecking from him... Shit.

"Oh," she murmured in a surprised tone as she angled her face from side to side. "I look...different."

"Like a petrified raccoon?" Hell yeah, he was digging for a compliment. He'd done good. He'd even done cat-eyes eyeliner on her like the stupid tutorials had shown him how to do.

"No. I look..."

"Beautiful."

Lynn looked at him in the mirror with wide, startled eyes, as if she was a deer in headlights. "I do?"

26

Jathan nodded. Yeah, the word "beautiful" was one of his manipulations, but he didn't care. The slow smile on her face said it worked well enough. He would give her a hundred compliments if it made her fight again. If she was stronger, he would've told her she looked hot and fuckable, just like he told the girls he was trying to sleep with in town when his bear became too much and needed sex to settle. Lynn was fragile though, so she would need pretty words. He was going to have to pretend to be a gentleman.

"Show me," she whispered.

But as he led her out of the tree house and down the narrow staircase to the field of dandelions below, her eyes went dead again, and she walked behind him like she was already a ghost.

THREE

Confused, Lynn squinted against the evening light, trying to focus. There was a wall of weeds in front of her. Big weeds, taller than her. What the hell?

She scanned the perfectly manicured yard, the neatly trimmed landscaping, and the fresh mulch that lined the front of the mobile home. The giant weeds made no sense here.

"Meet Henry," Jathan said from behind her.

She startled. She'd forgotten about Jathan and had been wondering if she'd sleepwalked here. She did that sometimes—woke up in strange places. Her panther took over and pushed her out, and she would end up in the woods or beside a road. Once she even ended up in someone's car because she'd apparently been hitchhiking.

Baffled, she asked, "Who is Henry?"

"The bigass weed in front of you. The tallest one."

Lynn arched her gaze to the top of the weed and shook her head. "Is this your den?"

"Yep. Home sweet home, right on the outskirts of Grayland Mobile Park. Singlewide, five years old, has two working window-unit air conditioners and only gets bugs in the summertime. It's a love shack. The ladies come a runnin' when they find out I live in this castle."

Lynn giggled, but it scared her, so she clapped her hand over her mouth.

Jathan's fingertips touched her lower back. "You should laugh more."

Sometimes he didn't make sense to her, so she changed the subject. "Why don't you pull the weeds. Everything else looks pristine."

"Pull the weeds? Woman, I grew these from baby-weeds! That was a tiny dandelion a month ago. I gave it plant food and I'm trying to get it as tall as me. It's a goal of mine."

"Well, it's good to have weird hobbies."

Jathan chuckled and splayed his hand across her lower back. His palm was huge. Big as a bear paw, even when he was human. Usually touch made her flinch away, but for some reason, she stayed right where she was, practically purring under his touch. Trouble, trouble, trouble.

"Where do you go?"

"Hmmm?" she asked, forcing her gaze away from Henry.

"When your eyes go dead and you stop talking...where do you go?"

Lynn gave a helpless shrug. "I don't know. I just...disappear."

"Mmm." He reached out and stroked a prickly leaf on Henry, almost as if he used the weed so he had another place to put his hand. Then he narrowed his eyes at her. "You want to know what I think?"

"Not really."

"Look, I took psychology one-oh-one in college, and I'm basically a professional. I think you disappear when you talk about, or think about, something that hurts. I think your panther thinks she's protecting you, but it messed you up instead."

Lynn clenched her fists at her sides and fought the tingling sensation in her middle that said she would Change soon. "You think too much about me. Best you stop that before you get attached to something that's a puff of smoke in the wind."

"Mmm," he said again. "You wanna fuck, Smoke Nut?"

Lynn sighed. "All boys are the same."

"Boys, yes, men, no."

"You're a man, not a boy?"

"I'm here, aren't I? Where's Brody? Hmm? Where's the boy who did this?"

Blink.

"No!" Jathan gripped her chin and pulled her gaze to his. "Nope, don't run, Smoke Nut."

Blink.

"Lynn!"

Blink.

She was trying to hold on, really she was, but Brody was something she couldn't think about. She couldn't because it hurt too much. "Jathan," she whispered as her vision collapsed inward. The sky went dark, and then the woods behind him. Everything was covered in shadows until only Jathan's worried, chocolate brown eyes were in focus. They were holding her, tethering her. If she could just stay here a little longer...

Blink.

Jathan's lips crashed onto hers. His hands went rough in the back of her hair as he forced her face against his. The kiss was a storm that jolted her from the cold, dead waters of the black ocean she'd tried to escape to. His mouth moved against hers in a violence that was breathtaking

32

and painful and perfect. His sharp teeth scraped her lip, and when she opened her eyes, the forest was there again behind him. It was dark, but there.

Desperate to anchor herself in this moment, she slid her hands up the strong planes of his chest, around his thick neck, and then tightened her arms around him.

"Stay," he ground out against her lips before he pushed his tongue into her mouth.

He tasted so good. His hands were steady against her back and in her hair. She waited for the trapped feeling, but it didn't come. Not when he dragged her closer, and not when he pushed her through the landscaping and pressed her back against the side of his trailer. Not when he lifted her up like she weighed nothing at all and rocked onto her pelvis just right.

Broken, broken Lynn, giving in to a man again. But this was different. Jathan wasn't Brody. He wasn't trying to lock her down, but was playing with her instead. Oh, she knew he was in this for the next six days because she was a safe bet. He wouldn't have to get attached. Men like Jathan didn't do bonds. They didn't do deep connections. He was a bad bear, and she was a bad kitty, and maybe for tonight, one of her last nights, she could feel something.

He rolled his hips against hers slowly, one, two, three, and she thought he would drag this out, but suddenly he pushed the pace. He was so powerful against her as he sped up, and oh, this felt so good. It had been so long since a man touched her like this. Since anyone touched her at all.

He bit her lip hard enough that she tasted iron, but she liked it. She liked rough. Wanted it. Wanted Jathan the way he was. Monster. He lowered his lips to her neck and sucked so hard she gasped in pleasure and pain.

"Are you still with me?" he growled against her skin.

"I'm here," she answered breathily. God, she was holding on so tight. *Don't leave, don't leave.*

Let me have this moment, Monster.

He slowed again, his erection pressing against her just right, teasing, changing the rhythm when she got close. Her toes were curled with how good it felt, and gooseflesh covered her skin. Oh, this man could fuck. She could tell from how he was revving up her body.

"More," she begged, reaching between them. He was strong like an oak, and he snarled a sexy sound when she pushed her fingertips into the front of his jeans. He was big, perhaps too big for her body, she didn't know yet, but she was willing to try. Willing to lose herself to a fun night just to get some relief from her head. Because he was doing it. He was distracting her from the turmoil inside of her, and she never wanted this to stop. She slid her hand down his pants farther and gripped his thick shaft. And then she grinned as he bucked into her hand and made a sexy groan in his throat. She'd been powerless for so long, and look here. She could pull a helpless noise from a someday alpha with a touch. For the first time in years, she was in control of something.

His lips collided with hers again, and he settled her on her feet, pressed her back against his home. The kiss was desperate. It wasn't romantic, or lovey dovey. It was two people who needed release as soon as possible to be okay.

Jathan gripped her hips and exhaled a breath as he rolled against her again. His hands were shaking slightly, and she loved this. The snap of his button sounded so loud in the quiet of the evening, and so did the quick rip of the zipper, but when she moved to shove his pants down his waist, he jerked away. "Fuck," he whispered, retreating a few steps. He ran his hand through his longer hair on top and paced away, then back through the landscaping to reach her. "We can't. You're not ready."

"Then I'll never be ready," she said, angry at being cut off. "This is as good as I get."

"Bullshit. This is rock bottom. I can't fuck you when you're at rock bottom."

Lynn huffed a pissed-off breath and looked away in shame. "Of course. Just like every other boy."

"Don't get it twisted. A boy would fuck you right now, Lynn. A man would wait until you're ready."

"You sleep with everyone," she gritted out. "Fuck." Something was happening to her face. Warmth trailed from her eyes to her cheeks and dripped off her jaw. She wiped the tears angrily and strode between the bushes, blasting past him. She needed to get out of here. Needed to hide because she was going to fall apart and she was going to disappear and she was going to Change and Monster would do awful things. She was going to fight. Who was next? Kirk? Beaston? Creed?

Help me! She wanted to scream it because she'd needed it so desperately all along. But with this thing that had happened to her, that had created her and made her unloveable, she had to be quiet. Suffer in silence, because who would understand? No one. If she admitted all her sins, who would still stand against her storm? Again, no one.

"Tell me why you're mad," Jathan demanded, keeping pace with her.

Which way was home? Which way to the tree house? *I can't breathe.*

"Tell me!"

A wave of power washed over her skin, and she went down to her knees automatically. He was doing what Ben did. What Greyson did. What Creed of the Gray Backs did. He was pulling rank and making her panther think he was alpha. Making her obey. Not fair. Not fair!

Jathan went to his knees in front of her and gripped her shoulders. "Tell me, and I'll give you relief."

Struggling to inhale, she choked out, "I just wanted to not feel broken for a little while."

"Touch fixes it?"

"I don't—I—" *Can't breathe!* "I don't know."

Jathan's eyes were two green, glowing flames

in the evening shadows as he scanned the woods. After a second of hesitation, he dragged her onto his lap, straddling her legs around his hips, and before she could react, he rucked her dress up, slipped his hand down the front of her panties and dragged his fingers through the wetness he'd conjured between her legs.

Lynn was panting for breath, but the tightness in her chest eased a little, and she wanted more. She wanted that steady feeling he'd given her against the house. "Please," she begged. "It doesn't mean anything. Just...fix me for a little while."

Jathan looked angry as he stared off into the woods and shook his head, but it only lasted a moment before he gripped the back of her neck with his free hand and kissed her, plunging his tongue into her mouth in the same moment he slid two fingers inside of her. She moaned into his mouth and melted against him.

He was keeping her here, keeping her present, not allowing her to disappear, and it had been so damn long since she felt this in control. He pulled his fingers out and pushed them back in, even deeper, and now she was rocking her hips with the pace he set. Her entire body was trembling, but it was with want, not fear, so she melted against him and hugged his neck as their lips moved against each other's.

This was safe. This was release without love. Love ruined everything, but Jathan was good for her. He was disconnected, too. He was Monster, too. She'd seen his bear. Their demons matched, and there was no chance at either one of them falling for each other before her time was up. She could enjoy his affection, his attention, his body, guilt free. *For once*, she could do something guilt-free. This was freedom from herself.

He smelled good. Fur and cologne and arousal, and she could feel his erection between her legs as she rocked against his touch. He didn't slow her down this time but pushed into her faster and faster until she was panting out his name. Until she was clawing at the back of his neck and fighting the urge to bite him on his exposed throat. Until she was shattering in an intense orgasm around his fingers. He pushed into her deep, over and over, until the throbbing felt unbearably good. Then it faded away, pulse by pulse.

And then he broke the unspoken rules.

Jathan cupped her cheek tenderly and kissed her like this wasn't desperation. He kissed her like he was adoring her, like he was coveting her. No. No, no, no, this wasn't how it was supposed to work. He was stirring up warmth in her chest. Stirring up these feelings that she wanted more gentleness, but that was the last thing she needed. Lynn needed rough to sate Monster, not adoration.

She flinched away from his kiss and pulled him by the wrist out from under her dress. "I'm hungry." And a little angry, but from his glare, he could probably tell that part.

"Get on my Harley," he gritted out.

Lynn gave him a wicked smile. "That's more

like it. I like when you boss me around. Don't like it when you try to make me fall for you. Remember always, love is fire. Love won't fix me. Play with my body, but leave my heart alone."

Lynn shoved off him and made her way to the Harley parked in front of his trailer. While she was straightening the hem of her dress, he slid a helmet over her head and startled her. Without a word, he gave her a devil-may-care smile, kicked a leg over his bike, and turned it on. The roar of it was so loud it vibrated through her chest.

What was this she was feeling when he cast her a green-eyed glance over his shoulder? Was it a trill of excitement? That seemed right. She was going to ride a motorcycle for the first time in her life. A hundred years ago, in another lifetime, she had dreamed of riding on the back of Jathan's bike. He'd had a motorcycle during his senior year in high school, and all the girls adored the Bad Bear. While he was preparing to graduate, she had only been a shy sophomore. She'd watched him quietly. Pined for him in silence, and now here she was, at the end of her life, and she was marking off a bucket list item.

Helmet fastened, she got on behind him, wrapped her arms around his waist, interlocked her fingers, and held on tight as he blasted them out of the yard. She couldn't catch her breath as he sped under the Grayland Mobile Park sign, or even when he hit the main road that led out of Damon's Mountains. It took her a minute to realize why—she was laughing.

Over his shoulder, Jathan said, "Lynn, don't let go of me. Are you still with me?"

"Yeah." Lynn held onto him tighter as they hit smooth asphalt. "I'm still here."

FOUR

It was crowded at Sammy's Bar. They weren't even inside yet, but she could tell by the gravel parking lot completely full of cars. There wasn't a single spot left.

Jathan had already gotten off his bike, which he'd parked right up front on the sidewalk, like he didn't care if he got towed at all. He was on the phone. "Because I don't *have* to pick up their calls, asshole. No...Jax, for fuck's sake, your crew calls me eighty times a day. I have a life, and I'm not supposed to even have my phone up on the job site. Yeah... Yes! Look, she's right here with me, still breathing. Lynn," he said, turning to her, "say hi. My dickhole brother wants proof of life."

"H-hi, Jax."

"Lynn!" Jax yelled through the line. "Lynn, fight girl. Come back to us. We fucking miss you! Eden is going crazy, so is Greyson, so are all of us. Just...get better!"

Jathan rolled his eyes and hung up on his twin brother. "Red Havoc is a crew of stage five clingers," he muttered, typing something into his phone.

His head was angled down as he frowned at the glowing screen. Jathan had good posture. He was a massive man, all muscles and broad shoulders and biceps the size of tree trunks that pressed against a black Harley Davidson T-shirt. Tattoos curled up his neck from his collar, and from under his short sleeves of his shirt. Down, down the ink went, all the way to his knuckles. He had even more than Jaxon did, and a very different style. Jathan's were more artwork, bigger pieces of geometric design, as though he'd treated his skin as a canvas. His forearms flexed as he texted away on his phone, and his bottom lip poked out slightly in a look of sexy concentration. He was as tall as a damn house, six-four, and he towered over her, but he wasn't clumsy with the extra stature. He was graceful, yet powerful. His muscular legs pressed against the material of his dark jeans, and the scuffed work boots on his feet were size gigantor. She'd felt his erection earlier and was now a firm believer in that joke about foot size and dick size. Jathan was big everywhere.

He slid her a glance, and she was relieved to find his eyes were darkened to his human color of soft brown. The look was quick and so was the curve of his lips. A fast smile, just for her. Huh. She usually made people uncomfortable. Not smiley.

"You gonna growl all night?" he asked. "I mean, it's sexy as fuck, but you might scare the humans inside."

Was she growling? Lynn swallowed the noise

down. "There are going to be a lot of people inside."

Jathan hit one final button on his phone and shoved it in his back pocket, straightened, and faced her in a motion that was all confidence. He lifted his chin and smiled down at her, his eyes cool. "It'll be fine. You used to come to Sammy's every weekend. Remember?"

"No." Lynn frowned and tried to recall her time in Damon's Mountains. She'd blocked a lot out after things started going wrong.

"Remember what it looks like inside?" he asked, holding out his hand to help her off the bike. His giant hand was calloused.

"Job site?" she asked.

Jathan surprised her when he kept up with her flighty train of thought. "I work with the Gray Backs now. I'm a logger."

"You're a lumberjack werebear," she said with a little giggle at the end.

"I am. The job suits me. It's hard work and wears out my animal." He grabbed her hand and pulled her off the bike. As he removed her helmet, he explained further, "I hate the weekends. I hate the off-season." He opened his mouth to say more, but hesitated, then frowned. "I don't know why I'm telling you this."

"Maybe because I'll take your secrets to my grave in six days," she teased.

He busied himself with hanging her helmet on the handlebars of his bike, but she'd seen the flash of anger on his face before he'd turned away.

"I hate weekends, and I hate the fire season, because it means I don't work out the bear as much as I need to. Those days I struggle to keep him under control. I'm not telling you because you have an expiration date, Lynn, and if you say that again, I'm gonna stay pissed and ruin the night. I don't want that, so don't joke about leaving."

"Dying," she said stubbornly. "Call it what it is."

He cast her a feral look over his shoulder and

flashed his teeth in a snarl. His eyes were muddy now as he rounded on her and gripped her shoulders. "I'm telling you about my bear because you called your panther Monster, and I call my animal the same damn thing. I'm telling you because you'll understand. I'm telling you so you get it through your thick head that you aren't alone. No more jokes about dying. Six days. Don't mention it again. We're going to pretend this isn't the end."

"Maybe I don't want to play that game," she said, crossing her arms over her chest.

"You don't have a choice."

Jathan grabbed her hand and pulled her toward the door so fast she had to jog to keep up. Oh, he was mad. She could tell from the tension in his back, pressing against the thin, black fabric of his T-Shirt. She could tell by how tight he was holding her hand, as if he didn't care whether he ground her bones to dust. She could tell from the snarl in his chest and the scent of his fury. Fur and motorcycle oil and anger. And whatever this said about her, she didn't care, but she thought he was sexy, all revved up and passionate like this.

The second she stepped foot inside, a hundred memories of Sammy's bombarded her. It was all dark wood floors, dark walls, and exposed rafters. There were old, rusty street signs on the walls, tables around a dance floor, and a stage on the right side where she'd watched countless shows by the Beck Brothers. The bar was in back, and Layla, Kong's mate, was talking to a human regular named Gus that she remembered from way back when. There were a dozen shifters in here she recognized from Damon's Mountains. Nothing had changed here, but everything had changed with her, and there was this sense of happiness and sadness all swirled into one overwhelming feeling inside of her chest.

Blink.

"Nope," Jathan murmured and leaned down just as the room started going dark. "Medusa," he whispered, and then he kissed her, but not the violent kind. It was one of those kisses where they just pressed their lips against each other and froze, connected only by a still touch. He waited a four-count, then pulled away with a soft smack, and God bless the man, he looked as confused as she felt by that kiss. But the room wasn't dark, so there was that.

"Shots," he muttered with a deep frown marring his dark eyebrows. "Shots and fried steak. Only the best on a date with me, Smoke Nut."

Lynn snorted and ended the noise with a laugh. "That's literally the worst pet name ever."

"Fine. Only the best for *my girl*." But the way he'd said *my girl* sounded hollow. It sounded like a lie.

He pulled her to a corner table that was occupied by two middle-aged men talking over a pitcher of beer.

"Fuck off," Jathan growled.

And fuck off, they did. Both men glared, but

they slid out of the booth, took their beer, and made their way to the bar.

"Does everyone do what you say?" she asked softly as she stared after them.

"Mostly. Not Jax, though."

"When you said 'my girl,' you lied. I'm not your girl." Lynn angled her head curiously as she watched him slide into the booth and wipe crumbs off the table with the flat of his palm. "Are you manipulating me?"

"Yep. Sit down so I can stare at your tits better. This angle is horrible for being a perv."

Well, at least the man was honest.

Lynn slid in across from him and pulled the V of her neck down lower. Her face was hurting again, which meant she was smiling, and now Jathan was staring at her lips, not the cleavage she'd just exposed. "Perv. Eyes down here, not up here," she said, swirling her finger at her face.

"Most girls want the opposite," he murmured, leaning back in the booth, brushing one outstretched leg against her ankle under the table.

"Your first mistake was thinking I'm like most girls." Whoa, where had that come from?

"Oooh! She knows how to flirt. That's hot, Smoke Nut. I'll be sure to stare inappropriately at your chest even when you're talking about serious stuff then."

She narrowed her eyes. "Serious stuff like what?"

"What is Red Havoc like?"

"Why do you want to know?"

The smile dipped from his face, and his eyes went serious. "Because my brother lives there now."

"Do you miss him?"

Jathan clenched his teeth hard and nodded to a passing waitress. She gave him the be-right-with-you wave. He cleared his throat and leaned forward, resting his elbows on the table. "Tell him this ever, and I'll deny it to the grave."

"Secrets are safe with a dead person, Jathan, remember?" Yeah, she was testing him, but if she was honest, she loved the pissed-off look he got when she talked about the coming end. When she left this world, Jathan would care, and having someone feel something about her passing was loosening something in her chest she hadn't realized had been so tight.

Jathan yanked her hand across the table and bit her wrist, almost hard enough to draw blood. It hurt. His green eyes were remorseless when he released her hand and leaned back again. Punishment administered, he admitted, "I miss my brother very much. He isn't just a sibling. He's a twin, and there is something special about the bond there. I hate him and I love him and I hate him and I love him on an endless loop. But I didn't ever really think we would belong to separate crews who lived so far away."

"But he was rogue for a long time."

"Yeah, but he came back to the Gray Backs for a few days at a time before he wandered again. He came back to me." Jathan shook his head. "Not anymore. He's happy with his mate, happy with

Red Havoc. Happy for the first time maybe, I don't know. It eats at me. It's something I'll never find, and sometimes I get angry that he did this huge life change without me."

"Jealous?"

"Yes," Jathan said without a second of hesitation. "Not of him finding a mate. That's horseshit, and we both know it. I'm jealous of him finding a way to settle his bear."

Lynn dipped her gaze to a tattoo on his flexed triceps. It was three lines of text.

This Love

This Hate

This Pain

She wanted so badly to ask about the meaning, but he caught her eye and angled his arm away from her in an obvious shut-down. "Your turn. Tell me about my brother's crew. Tell me about the new C-Team, as he calls it. Tell me about your life in Red Havoc."

The waitress bustled up right as Lynn was about to deny him. Thinking about home made her sad right now, and she wanted to keep her body.

Jathan ordered them two waters, four shots of tequila, and two chicken fried steak plates. She'd never had a man order for her, and though she was independent, it felt kind of nice not having to talk to a stranger when she was already struggling to keep herself. Jathan had just taken care of it...taken care of her.

Lynn crossed her arms over her chest and leaned back against the booth. Interesting man...

Fine. Since he shared about his brother, she would give him happy stuff. Nothing painful so she wouldn't slip back into the dark, so she could stay here...with him.

"I lived in the second cabin from the front. It's tiny, and inside, I painted the logs light purple. Ben got so mad when he saw what I'd done, but purple is my favorite color, and I always wanted to live in purple rooms."

Jathan leaned forward again, a slight smile on his lips as if he was enjoying story time. "Did you piss your alpha off a lot?"

"Every chance I got. Why do you look surprised?"

"Because when you lived here, you were a goody-goody. You wouldn't even sneak out with us."

"Yeah, well I was trying to get myself adopted." Lynn frowned at herself. Where had that come from? Usually when she thought of hard stuff, she disappeared.

"I remember. It took three years, but it happened. The day you and your parents went to court to sign those final papers and make it official? The Gray Backs celebrated."

"They did?"

"Yeah. We had this huge barbecue. We invited you, but your parents said they wanted to do a private celebration, just the three of you. We understood..." He gave her a devilish grin, "But we used it as an excuse to party anyway. My mom made this bigass sign in rainbow letters that said *Congrats on not being an orphan anymore.'"* Jathan laughed to himself and rolled his eyes. "It was hideous. You would've hated it."

"No," she murmured, "I would've loved that."

"It's probably still in the storage trailer. I can find it if you want."

The waitress set down their waters and shots. Jathan handed her one and then lifted one of his own. "To rebellious purple walls. Fight everything." He tinked his tiny glass against hers, and they both touched the bottoms to the table, then tossed back the shot.

God, how long had it been since she had done this? Her throat burned as the liquor worked its way down. The long sound of a single guitar note rang out and then wrenched up an octave as someone tuned it. Up on stage, Denison and Brighton Beck of the Ashe Crew were getting ready to perform.

"Did you know the Beck Brothers were playing tonight?" she asked.

"Yep. Told you. Only the best for my girl." *My girl* didn't sound quiet as false now, and that confused her.

"More," he demanded, handing her another shot.

"More tequila?"

"No, more Red Havoc. And tequila. Your turn to toast now, Smoke Nut."

She giggled and lifted the shot. "To the worst pet name in the world."

"Here, here."

Together they slammed the shots, and then Jathan pushed her water toward her. "Rehydrate between every two shots so you don't get sick tonight."

Huh. That was surprisingly sweet of him to care about her night like that. Most boys would've gone hard at getting her drunk.

As if he could read her mind, he stopped sipping his own water and said, "I don't need you drunk to fuck you, Lynn. You'll say yes either way. You'll beg, and I'll consider it, but only if you aren't drunk." He flicked his fingers at her glass. "Water."

She glared at him, unsure of how to respond. She'd never liked men telling her what to do in general, but when Jathan did it, he was so sure she would listen, and that confidence was sexy. In a way, she wanted to listen to him. She wanted to please him. He didn't have to know that though. "Bossy," she accused.

"And a big reason I'm not made to pair up with a woman. I like tough girls, but who would put up with my shit? Hmm?"

Uh, a lot of women, because he was hot-as-sin, well-spoken, had a steady job, had a house, paid his own bills, loved his family, would probably be alpha of a crew someday, and when he was bossy, he was bossy with good intentions. He was brutally honest. *And* he rode a Harley. Did she mention the hot-as-sin part? She wasn't really seeing a downside to Jathan Barns.

"I think for the next six days, maybe I need a boss."

"Mmm," he practically purred as he angled his head back and looked down at her. "I like when your voice goes all sexy like that. You like being bossed, Lynn? We can play that game. It's my favorite kind."

She sipped her water again to stall until she knew her voice wouldn't come out a horny squeak when she spoke. After clearing her throat delicately, she said, "I don't think I would like it if anyone else bossed me right now. Not my alpha in Red Havoc, not any man. But it feels different with you. Maybe I could use some games this week." Especially from a hot boy who knew his way around women, a man who wouldn't get attached to a girl like her.

Jathan was safe. Safe, safe, safe. Only a Bad Bear would do for the kind of distraction she needed this week.

The food arrived, along with two more shots of tequila with limes, and when she followed Jathan's gaze to the bar, she waved her thanks to the giant gorilla shifter behind the register. Kong nodded his chin and mouthed, *Welcome back.*

Something warm and fuzzy and annoying

unfurled in Lynn's chest. She wasn't doing very well at being invisible here.

The first song from the Beck Brothers rang out, a country crooner, and she poured extra gravy all over her fried steak. Feeling reckless as a hellion, she said, "I moved to the Red Havoc Crew for a boy. Brody. I found him online, and he was perfect on paper. A panther like me, and charismatic, and funny, and attentive, and rebellious. When I got up the courage to contact him, he responded like I was the only girl in the world worth knowing. He worked me relentlessly. Persued me. I was so lonely at the time, I got addicted to his attention. He had just joined the Red Havoc Crew and he said I should join to, so we could be together. So I joined. I packed up my entire life and moved far away from everything I'd known. For him."

The sound of Jathan's silverware hitting the plate as he set them down was louder than the music. Carefully, he cracked his knuckles and clenched his hands in front of his mouth. "And?"

"And, you know."

"I know what my brother told me."

As she looked him in the eyes, Lynn tried to smile and look strong, but her lips trembled. "And for a while it was perfect, and we were dating, and then Brody fell in love with another girl in the crew. A girl who had become my friend. Her name is Winter. She didn't know how much I cared for him when they bonded, because Brody had always stressed the importance of us being secretive and quiet about us so we wouldn't feel pressure from other people about the pace of our relationship. But with Winter, he came right out with his feelings and let the entire crew know she was his. I felt broken everyday watching them, and then one day, it changed. Brody gave me attention again, and it got easier. It was everything I'd dreamed of it being. Even better than it had been before, and this time he was open with our relationship. I felt wanted, and important to him. I'd waited for him to come back, and then he was telling me he'd made a mistake with Winter, that he'd broken off their bond, that he was leaving her to be with me, and everything got really complicated. Everything but my heart, which belonged to Brody." The lights above were dimming, and she wouldn't be able to stay this time. Couldn't. So she rushed on so that Jathan could see how horrible a person she was before she went vacant again. "He bonded to me while he was still bonded to Winter. He lied to us both, but it's my fault. I wanted it so bad. Wanted someone to love me because my parents had thrown me away when I was seven, Jathan. They had raised me for seven years before they put me up for adoption. I couldn't get them to love me, and then I had to try so hard to get my foster parents to keep me. I felt like no one would ever care about someone like me. Like I was born a disappointment. So when Brody, the man I'd wanted for so long, offered me what I thought was love...I betrayed Winter, my friend, for him. And I'll never, ever forgive myself for that first big sin."

Blink. Time was lost.

FIVE

Heart banging against his sternum, hands clasped in front of his face, chest heaving with his shaking breath, Jathan watched the light fade from Lynn's pretty brown eyes. She'd just leveled him to nothing with her admission.

Oh, he'd known she'd broken up Brody and Winter, now of the Blackwing Crew, but he hadn't realized she'd been there first. He hadn't realized she'd loved Brody before Winter was in the picture, and he sure as shit hadn't realized she was carrying that guilt. He'd done his research on her starting the day he brought her back to Damon's Mountains because he'd wanted to know what made a tough-girl panther shifter like Lynn go all pathetic.

He'd been so. Fucking. Wrong.

She wasn't pathetic at all. He knew some of her story, knew it had gotten worse for her, but he'd blamed her for making bad decisions. Blamed her for being weak. And sure, she had made bad decisions, but not because she was a bad person. She'd had reasons he couldn't have guessed at until now. She had drowned in this idea of belonging, being wanted, and feeling loved. And instead of getting angry at Brody for what he'd done, Lynn blamed herself.

A broken mating bond hadn't killed the old Lynn...

Guilt had.

Jathan cast a quick glance around, but nobody was paying attention to them. His food was getting cold, but screw it. He couldn't stomach eating while she sat here staring vacantly ahead, smelling like fur and sadness. He slid to the other side of the booth and sat right next to her. And then he gave two middle fingers to the coward inside of him because she would never remember what he was about to do. He pulled her against his chest and rested his chin on the top of her head. And rocking gently, he just held her.

Lynn would hate this if she was awake. She balked against tenderness and wanted only rough so she could pretend she didn't have feelings. It was a coping mechanism so she could keep calm in the last six days.

Well, fuck six days, and fuck keeping it easy for her to leave.

She was going to live, even if he had to fight every single alpha who tried to put her down.

With her admission, she'd changed the game. She wasn't Crazy Lynn to him anymore.

She was Broken Lynn who needed one person to really believe in her. One person to stand up for her. One person to be patient with her. One person to get her fighting again.

And she could fight. He knew she could. Why? Because tonight, she'd played, wanted touch, and tried to stay present with him. She'd flirted, told jokes, and agreed to come to a crowded bar just to live a little. If she didn't care about life, she would've checked out and still have been sitting vacantly up in that treehouse, etching another mark onto her wall when she came to.

Fuck six days.

He was going to give her thousands.

SIX

Lynn blinked hard as the blurry edges of her vision slowly came into focus.

Where the hell was she?

Some kind of bathroom. Looked familiar. Sterile looking, white tiles covered the walls, beige tiles covered the floor, and there was the same mirror that was in the women's restroom at...Sammy's Bar. On the counter sat a tiny redheaded woman in a red plaid mini-skirt, knitting an oddly-shaped blanket. Her legs were crossed, and she looked comfortable enough. She shoved her glossy, black horn-rimmed glasses up her nose and went back to knitting. Why was she even wearing glasses? Shifters had impeccable vision. And on further inspection, Willa's glasses didn't have any lenses in them.

Baffled, Lynn looked down at her lap. She was sitting in a chair with a warm, purple-pomegranate beer in one hand and a penis straw in the other. What the hell?

"I thought you would be thirsty, and sometimes fruity beers taste better with a straw. Look." Willa Barns lifted up the blanket she was knitting. "It's a dick rug. I'm making it for Jathan's house. He will hate it, and I will laugh and laugh."

Indeed, it looked like a pink erect penis and balls.

"W-where is Jathan?"

"Outside bleeding that wanker, Nox. They're playing punchy punchy face face, and I figured you wouldn't want everyone staring at you so I brought you in here. Plus, my son said he would poison my red wigglers—those are worms—if I didn't watch after you while he took Nox out back to bleed him. And he would, too. We're in the middle of a prank war, and my boy doesn't play fair. He's a total dick." Willa gave a Grinch-like smile. "I love him."

"Cool. Why is he fighting Nox?" Yep, she was concerned. Nox, aka the son of the Cursed Bear, aka Clinton's son, aka total psychopath, was a beast. She knew. She'd fought him for just that reason.

"Oh, he and Nox fight every few days. They hate each other."

There was a knock on the bathroom door, which was apparently locked.

"Who is it?" Willa yelled at an uncomfortable volume.

"Uuuuh, Julie?"

Willa sighed and mouthed, *So human.* "Entry denied. Go use the boy's bathroom please and thank you!"

"Um, why do Jathan and Nox hate each other?"

"Because who doesn't hate Nox? He got one-hundred-unfortunate-percent of his father's DNA and pisses everyone off on purpose. He came in here looking for a fight, so Jathan is giving him one."

Another knock sounded.

"Not today, Julie!"

"Ma, let me in."

It was Jathan's growly voice on the other side, and suddenly a trill of excitement ran through Lynn at the prospect of seeing him. Uh oh. Well, that wasn't good. She couldn't afford to get attached now. She needed to lock her feelings down, and quick.

She mentally prepared herself to look nonchalant as Willa scrambled to unlock the door and let in her son, but when Jathan ducked under the doorframe and locked eyes with her, Lynn's heart rate kicked up double-time. He had a cut under his eye, crimson streamed down one cheek, and his knuckles were battered, cut, and bloody. He was bruising already.

"Aw, don't look at me like that, Lynn. You

should see the other guy."

"Is he alive?" Willa asked, studying Jathan's torn-up knuckles.

"Unfortunately. Ma, stop fussin'." He eased his hand from Willa's and ran it under the tap water. It was cute watching tiny Willa worrying over her giant, behemoth, badass son. And it was really sweet the way he let her rest her cheek on his shoulder. After a couple of seconds, he relaxed and pressed his cheek on top of her bright red hair. Willa huffed suddenly, tossed her dick rug over her shoulder, pocketed the knitting needles, and said, "Try harder to kill him next time. He's getting on everyone's damn nerves. Good night, you two." She headed for the door while she was talking. "Lynn, it's good to see you again, ya little nut job. Make bad decisions tonight."

As the door closed behind the petite Almost Alpha of the Gray Backs, Lynn stood and set her fruity beer on the sink along with the penis straw. "Let me see," she murmured, ripping a handful of paper towels from the dispenser.

"I'm fine." He winced away from her touch on his cheek. "Lynn, I'm serious, it's fine."

She put water on the towels and persisted though. He wasn't the only one who had a stubborn streak.

With a snarl in his chest, he settled his butt against the counter and glared at the wall behind her with lightened, bright green eyes. But as she cleaned the drying blood from his face, he relaxed little by little, and more than once, she caught him looking down at her. As soon as he was busted though, he would give his attention to the wall again. "I have a theory," he finally murmured.

"Uh oh," she murmured. "Let's hear it."

"I think you carry too much guilt." He punched a number into his phone.

"What are you doing?"

"Easing it."

A ring sounded over the speaker phone, and she pulled the soaking paper towel away from his face. "Jathan! What are you doing?" she asked again, panicking. Something bad was happening.

"Hello?" Winter Donovan, Lynn's old friend, answered.

"Oh my God," Lynn whispered, tears instantly burning her eyes. She arched her gaze to Jathan. "Why would you do this?" She was so hurt by his betrayal. The bathroom was getting darker already. She'd just woken up, and he was putting her back to sleep.

Blink.

Jathan gripped her hair and forced her to look up at him. "Not yet. Fix this."

Bossy, bossy, bad bear. "You're bad," she said through the tears streaking down her face.

Jathan shrugged like he gave zero shits about that.

"Hello?" Winter asked again.

"Winter? It's Lynn," she said in a tiny voice.

"Lynn? Are you okay?"

"No." God, she felt gutted admitting that out loud. It was her first time admitting she wasn't

76

okay.

The panther in her middle writhed, scratching at her skin. She didn't want to do this, didn't want to do this, didn't want to do this. With a sob for the pain at fighting the Change, Lynn gripped the edge of the counter and went down. She knelt on the tile floor, curled over the ache. "Winter, I'm so sorry."

Jathan sat on the dirty bathroom floor, one big, strong hand on her thigh, the phone held close to her face with the other.

"Winter, I didn't mean to hurt you. I mean with Brody. I loved him before you came to Red Havoc and fell for him. I moved to Ben's crew for him because I thought he was it for me."

"Ooooh, honey," Winter murmured. "I forgave you for everything a long time ago. Do you want to know why?"

Lynn clasped her hand over her mouth to keep her sobs in her throat. She nodded like Winter could see her.

"You taking Brody was the best thing to

happen to me. It didn't feel like it at the time. I felt betrayed and hurt, but I hadn't really bonded to him. You forced me to make big changes in my life, and now I'm happier than I've ever been…with Logan. He's my match, my mate, the other half of me. I'm gonna have a baby, Lynn. A cub. Three more months. The doctor says we're having a little boy."

Lynn broke down. Shoulders shaking, she pitched forward, and rested her forehead on Jathan because it's all she could do. Winter was pregnant, happy, and had found her other half. Lynn could go knowing she'd turned out okay despite what she'd done to her.

"I heard what Brody did to you." Winter sniffed. "I'm the one whose sorry, Lynn. We both got hurt and lied to by that man. I know things can never be the same with us, but you're still my friend. And you'll always be a part of my story. The apology wasn't needed, but it means the world that you gave it."

All Lynn could do was cover her face with her

hands and try her best not to break apart. She didn't know what this feeling was in her middle. The pain of a Change? Was she disappearing again? No...it was something she hadn't felt in so long.

This feeling was relief.

"Thank you for forgiving me," she rasped out.

"Of course. Come visit me someday, Lynn. Come see where I ended up. My hope is that you end up in the same place."

Lynn clutched onto Jathan's shirt as he wrapped his arms around her and dragged her into his lap. This was the tragic part. The part where an old friend wished her a good life without knowing Lynn was at the end of what she could manage. She didn't want to do goodbyes yet though, so she let Winter keep that charitable thought.

"I'm sure we'll meet again someday," Lynn murmured. "Goodnight, Winter."

Blink.

Blink.

Blink.

But nothing happened. She stayed right where she was, in Jathan's lap, all hugged up in his strong arms, barely able to breathe from his embrace, tears streaming down her face as part of the impossible weight lifted from her shoulders.

There was no beauty in breaking. This man was witnessing the ugliest side of her.

But despite a peek at her damage...Jathan was still here.

Blink.

And so was she.

SEVEN

Two hours of sleep on a rock in the woods wasn't going to cut it today. Already, Creed had been on his case about how slow he was hooking the cables to the logs that littered the side of the mountain, but it was either take it slow and easy or make a mistake that could get one of the crew hurt. The parts of his mind that weren't totally exhausted were trained on Lynn. Sexy cat. She'd let him slide his hand up her thigh in the truck on the way home. She'd hinted she wanted him to come up to the tree house but, apparently deciding to be a gentleman for the first time in his whole stupid life, he declined.

When she'd gone vacant, he'd carried her up the stairs, tucked her into bed, and then like an idiot, sat outside her treehouse, on a rock, freezing his balls off. Why? Because he couldn't stay and be strong enough to tell her no a second time if she asked when she came to. But he couldn't leave her either. Not while she was checked out and all alone up there. Sleeping on a rock because he thought she wasn't ready for sex. What the fuck was wrong with him? He shouldn't care like this. It was terrifying.

"Jathan Daniel Barns!" Dad yelled from up on the landing. "Get your head out of your ass, son, or I'm gonna come down there and remove it for you! For fuck's sake, you are slowing literally everyone down. Tie up the logs and quit staring off into space!"

When Jason of the Gray Backs and his son Shane chuckled beside him, he wanted to stick his middle fingers and middle toes up at them. "Thanks a lot, Dad," he muttered.

"What did you say?" Dad barked from above.

"I said I'm about three milliseconds from quitting if you don't quit riding my ass. We're on pace for numbers, I'm keeping us steady, and no one has died today, so give me a fucking break!"

Dad lowered his chin to his chest and arched his eyebrows. "Boy, do you want to go?" He took off his work gloves and held out his hands, palms up. "I'm ready when you are. Just because you're grown, don't mean you're grown!"

"What?" Shane asked, a smile in his voice. "That doesn't even make any fucking sense."

"I always make sense!" Dad yelled.

Jathan made a tick sound behind his teeth, lifted his middle finger high, and hopped off the massive log he was standing on. Muttering about quitting any minute now like he did every day that ended with a Y, he yanked the cable around the log, fastened the hook to secure it, and turned to find Shane and Jason already had their logs done. Apparently, everyone had downed an entire pot of coffee this morning because both of them were smiling like cheerful little pecker-faces, and Jathan wanted to punch their stupid teeth out.

"You look like hell, man," Shane said as they hopped across logs like nimble mountain goats.

"Thanks a lot," Jathan muttered as he gestured for Creed to haul the trio of logs up to the landing so Dad could reach them with the processor. "I can't freaking wait to get done with this hill so I can get in a tree feller, turn up the music, and not have to talk to you dipshits anymore. You're exhausting."

"Or you're exhausted because you were out chasing tail all night." Shane's dark eyes danced as he propped a work boot up on a tree stump in the shade of a pine. He waggled his eyebrows and murmured, "Pussy tail."

Jathan shoved him hard. "Fuck off."

"You riding the crazy train now, Jathan? Cause everyone saw you with Crazy Lynn at Sammy's, and you're the talk of the trailer parks now. I mean, it's kind of messed up to fool around with a girl off her rocker, but me? I say all girls are off their rockers, so go get your dick wet."

Jathan slammed his fist into Shane's jaw before he could stop himself. His rage was so acute, he felt nothing as his knuckles blasted into him, and nothing when Shane was pummeling him back either. End over end, they fell down the damn mountain, latched onto each other. Jathan didn't care at all if he broke bones right now so long as Shane paid for talking about Lynn like that.

"She ain't crazy!" he gritted out, grunting as his back hit a stump and stopped their freefall.

"She fights every damn shifter in these mountains for funsies, asshole. She's crazy!"

"Then so am I!"

"Agreed. Ooof!" Shane hunched in on himself when Jathan socked him in the gut.

Warmth trickling down his split lip, Jathan shoved off him hard and made to walk away, got re-pissed off, and kicked him in the side, then flipped him off, then spat red on a tree stump and limped up the hill, ignoring the pain in his back because that would be healed before he even reached the landing.

"What the fuck has gotten into you?" Creed asked, his eyes round as Jathan stomped past him.

"I'm takin' a half day off."

"The fuck you are, get to work!"

"Creed! I haven't taken a single day off work since I started this job. I've never called in hungover, or taken a vacation, but I'm taking one now. I have five days to save her." God, where had that come from? He was telling Creed too much.

Creed's face morphed into one of shock. "You're making a run at saving Lynn?"

"Aren't you?"

Creed sighed and then shrugged one shoulder up. "She isn't like my other troubled shifters, Jathan. Ben told me before I even took her on that she's too far gone. She doesn't want to be saved. Five more days, and he'll be heading here to...you know."

"Put her down? Yeah, I know, Creed. It's all I've been able to think about for the last three weeks. I know there are shifters who have to be put down, but because they are dangerous to humans. She's not."

"She bleeds everyone who gives her half the chance, Jathan. She's totally snapped."

"False, she's salvageable."

"You're seeing what you want to see, but I'm watching her too, and I've done this before. I'm not scared of taking on the troubled shifters, Jathan, but this one is different. There's too much damage, and she isn't fighting anymore. Have you seen inside her home? She's counting down the days like she can't wait for this to be over." Creed shook his head sadly. "Sometimes it's more merciful to put a shifter down then let it go on."

Jathan felt like he'd been punched in the stomach. He wanted to puke just listening to

Creed quit on her. "You can't tell me you were able to help Beaston and my dad, but not Lynn. Fuck you for quitting on her. And fuck Ben for not being a good enough alpha for her."

Creed sighed and stared off into the woods. "Ben ain't alpha anymore. Power shifted in Red Havoc. It's Greyson McCarty runnin' that crew now."

"Since when?"

"Since the week before you picked Lynn up. Answer their damn calls, and maybe they would've told you. Why do you look mad?"

"Because the plan was to get her back to Red Havoc, Creed, but they just had a power shift, and you know as well as I do they'll be unsteady for a while yet. She needs calm waters."

Creed arched one dark eyebrow up. "Because you're an expert on rehabbing broken shifters?"

"Tell me I'm wrong," Jathan dared his alpha.

Creed ran a hand down his jaw and then hooked his hands on his hips. "Damon wants to talk to you."

"For what?" Jathan asked suspiciously. The ancient dragon shifter didn't summon the people in his mountains for tea and crumpets. An invite to the dragon's lair meant Jathan had probably messed up. Again.

"Hell if I know what he wants, I'm not his secretary. If you want that half day off, fine. We'll probably get work done faster without you and your piss mood anyway. But do me a favor and go see Damon first so he'll stay off my ass. He's called me three times this morning, and it's not like I can ignore calls from him. He's a fire-breathing dragon. I like my skin where it is and not extra crispy."

"Fine," Jathan muttered, climbing a pair of logs to make his way to the landing at the top of the hill.

"Jathan?" Creed asked.

He stopped and turned. "What?"

"I don't think you should get your hopes up."

"Why not?"

"Because listen."

Jathan shook his head in confusion. "To what?"

"Just...listen."

Off in the distance, there was a panther scream. Shit.

"She's fighting again. Maybe you had a good night, I don't know. Maybe you gave her a minute of relief, but her animal has completely snapped, man. I've been watching her, and she hasn't given one sign of being salvageable. And that's all I've been waiting for. One sign."

"Who? Who is she fighting today?"

"She's up in Boarland Mobile Park testing Harrison."

Jathan huffed a breath of relief. No shot in hell of Harrison losing control and giving her a kill bite. He would be playing defense only. He didn't like fighting female shifters.

"Like I said, I don't think you should get your hopes up...but..." Creed leveled him with those dark eyes of his, and his words went completely serious. "If you can find me one sign, I'll back you and do anything I can, including buy her time. Save her, Jathan. Because you and I both know she ain't motivated to save herself."

"What can I do?" he asked. "What did you do for Beaston? For my dad?"

"I gave them anchors and hoped they could hold on until they found something big enough to fight for."

Jathan already knew the answer, but he asked anyway. "And what were those?"

"Beaston found Aviana, and your dad found your mom." Creed canted his head and gave him one last look before he turned and gave a shrill whistle to Jason and Shane to start hooking logs to the skyline again.

Creed was saying she needed a mate, someone to fight for, and Jathan wanted to laugh. He didn't believe in mate bonds, didn't believe in settling with one person, didn't even believe in love. He'd never felt it. He'd always been half dead inside, an adrenaline junkie who hoped if he did enough wild living, drinking, sex, riding his motorcycle too fast, then never getting attached to anything would be okay, because he could convince himself he was the one living, not the shifters who had paired up.

Fuck. Creed thought Lynn needed a mate? She'd had one and now look at her, and Jathan was the only prospect now. Hands down, he was the worst choice for her. She needed sensitivity, gentleness, caring...and he was...him. He was a stone when she needed a feather mattress to land on.

But he also felt like her last shot because no one else was stepping up. No one cared like he did. They'd quit on her, and he wasn't even close to quitting. Why? Because last night she'd apologized to Winter for what she'd done, and then she'd fallen apart in his arms until she was out of tears. There was healing in that. Lynn had made a step in the right direction, so okay, he needed to give her anchors until she wanted to fight.

The panther screamed again. Beautiful

monster.

He was going to give her so many fucking anchors, she would never think of leaving without a fight again.

"Where are you going?" Dad called down from the massive processor perched on the edge of the landing.

"To see Damon."

"Oh. Well, don't die, son, your mother would be pissed."

"Glad you care, Dad," Jathan called.

"Glad you aren't a total screw up, just mostly one."

Jathan snorted because this was their game. It always had been. Right now, if he turned around, Dad would be staring at him with an obnoxious grin.

"I only love you sometimes," Jathan called over his shoulder.

"Same! See you at dinner! It's Taco Tuesday, and your mom is probably going to make them inedible."

T. S. JOYCE

"Can't wait!" Jathan gave a private grin, yanked open the door to his truck, and got in.

Every Tuesday was the same. Tacos were basically impossible to screw up, but Ma had a talent. That, and she liked to make up weird recipes. Last week, she served s'mores and tuna fish tacos, which were just as gross as they sounded. Dad usually ordered a pizza before Ma was even done cooking for their weekly family dinner. Tonight...Jathan was bringing Lynn because it was time for date number two, and Lynn needed some fun in her life. Plus, a tiny part of him had liked seeing Ma care for Lynn yesterday when she was checked out at Sammy's. Ma was tough, and Lynn could use strong women in her corner. Nah, that was bullshit. He'd liked them together for a different reason that he would never admit out loud. His two favorite girls were getting along.

Music up, windows down, thoughts on Lynn, always on Lynn, he made his way up the winding roads and steep switchbacks to Damon's house.

The dragon's mansion was built into a steep cliff, and beside it was a towering waterfall, feeding a stream that wound through the Mountains. There were long scorch marks on the cliff from a dragon war that had happened a few decades ago. Damon's lair had been destroyed, but he had rebuilt it. Jathan didn't know why he'd left the scorch marks on the cliff, but he would've done the same. He would've wanted the reminder that shifters were never really safe. He would've wanted the reminder to stay wary.

In the cup holder of his truck, his cell phone rang with the annoying ringtone of his brother Jaxon burping the words "A, B, C, D is for dick, and that should've been your naaaaaaame." His idiot brother had changed his ringtone to this last year. Jathan had acted mad at the time, but really, he sort of loved it and would never change it.

"Why the fuck didn't you tell me power shifted in the Red Havoc Crew?" Jathan answered as he glared at the waterfall.

Jax snorted. "Nice to talk to you too, broski. And I didn't tell you because you didn't ask. It's crew business. I don't ask you about Gray Back shit."

"Cop-out answer, *twin*."

"About that, Ma called and assured me you're adopted. There's no way she could've had a normal son like me and a weird one like you."

Jathan rolled his eyes. "We are identical, and Ma had no shot in hell at having normal children. What do you want? I'm about to head into Damon's house."

"Ew. Well, before you die, I have to tell you Ma really did call me."

"And? Ma calls me like seven times a day, and she lives three trailers away from me. Do you want a trophy for having a relationship with our parent?"

"All right, you sensitive little crybaby, Ma said you're about to go through hell, but when I pushed for answers, all she said was 'Lynn,' and then she hung up. Jathe...you okay?"

Jax only called him Jathe when he was serious or worried. Jathan relaxed against the headrest. "I'm going to be, and so will Lynn."

Jax let off a shaky breath. "You gonna bring her home?"

Gripping the steering wheel, he bit the corner of his lip then murmured, "I'm gonna try. Greyson taking alpha…I don't know him. Is he good?"

"Yeah. I expected fireworks when he took over the crew, but Ben rolled over on it. He was tired, and he and Jenny have another cub on the way. They just found out. He's happy to not have the weight of this crew on him, and Greyson is a badass. He's steady. Gotta good mate. The transition has been as smooth as it could be. The only problem? We're all feeling Lynn's absence. It's weird. I haven't seen her as a part of this crew since I moved out here, but even I feel the hole. Everyone is getting quieter and quieter as we get closer to the deadline. We're hurtin', man. If you can fix this? You'll have the fealty of the

Red Havoc Crew. Greyson told me as much this morning when I told him about Ma's call. You haven't been answering our calls, but I know you. If you didn't care, you would've been answering and telling us to fuck off, she's fine. But since you aren't, I think you care more than you let on, and she isn't okay, so you don't want to admit that to anyone. Am I right?"

No point in lying because Jax knew him better than anyone. "Yeah. You're right."

"God, Jathe, do you care for her?"

"Of course. She's hurting and she's from here. Of course I care if she is going to be one of the shifters who gets put down."

"No, that's not what I asked. Do you *care* for her?"

When Jathan gripped the steering wheel even harder, it creaked under his hand. He wasn't answering this. He didn't even know what all the feelings churning in his chest meant.

"No answer just told me the answer, Jathe. You're gonna freak out. You will. You always do.

You get close to a girl just a little bit, and then you run. You can't on this one."

"I know."

"No, man. Listen to what I'm saying. If you run, it will set off a chain of events that will hurt your crew and mine for always."

"I'm not running. I'm in this, and I don't need your pressure, Jax. I'm putting enough on myself here. I've got her."

"Jathe—"

"I said I've got her." There was movement at Damon's front door, and Jathan muttered a soft curse as he locked eyes with Beaston. The seer of the Gray Backs nodded a stone-faced greeting, then gestured him to the door. "I've got to go. I'll call you soon."

"I miss you," Jax blurted out.

Those three words hurt. They felt like three different slashes of a knife in his chest. It took him a few seconds to steady out and respond. "I miss you, too. Really bad. I could use you here right now, but I know you have your own life now. I'll call you soon." Jathan ended the call quick before his brother could respond. He needed to be tough in this meeting with Beaston and the dragon, and he couldn't be if Jaxon made him sentimental.

After a steadying three-count breath, Jathan shoved open his door and made his way up the marble walkway, up the stone stairs to the sprawling set of ancient wooden double doors with dragon's head knockers. Beaston's eyes were bright green, and there was no trace of smile lines on his face, as if he'd never smiled in his life. His arms were crossed over his chest, and he was leaned against the wall, one leg bent, one locked against the marble floor.

"What's happening?"

"Two things. Come on." Beaston twitched his head and led him inside.

Mason, Damon's boar-shifter assistant, was waiting inside, hands clasped behind his back formally. He'd turned logger for a couple decades with the Boarlander Crew but was back to spending days with his best friend, the blue dragon. Mason was an easy-going man, but right now, his smile didn't exist either.

It was cold in here and dim despite the chandeliers that adorned the ceiling. Mason led him and Beaston straight through the foyer and down a long, wide hallway lined with suits of armor. The metal masks of the knights were all fearsome animal faces. Bears, boars, tigers, dragons, ravens, lions, and more. When he was a kid, this place used to creep him out, and if he was honest, even now, at six-foot-four, built like a barn and not afraid of much, it still creeped him out.

Mason shoved open the double doors to Damon's office. The dragon himself sat behind his desk, signing paperwork. He looked up, and Jathan's blood cooled as the dragon shifter leveled him with those lightened silver eyes with the elongated pupils. Everyone's animals were worked up. This was bad.

"Have a seat," the dragon said, jerking his

chin to one of the chairs in front of his massive mahogany desk.

"I would rather stand. I'm not gonna lie, this feels a little bit like I've been called to the principal's office. Except I know I haven't done anything this time to warrant getting in trouble. I have somewhere to be. Make this quick. Please."

Damon narrowed his eyes and looked a little on the terrifying side, but Jathan crossed his arms over his chest and stood his ground. He should be in the Boarland Mobile Park right now, carrying Lynn's exhausted panther back to her treehouse, not playing head games with the three douche-keteers of these mountains.

"Have you heard from my son?" Damon asked.

Well that was unexpected. "No. Vyr isn't much of a phone talker. I'm sure you've noticed. The most I get is a perverted meme every once in a while, but he hasn't texted me in a few weeks. Not since he and Torren went after the gorillas in Red Havoc Territory."

Damon let off a sigh that turned into a room-shaking rumble. Anyone else would've pissed their pants in fear at the deep, chest-pulsing prehistoric sound, but he'd grown up in these mountains around the fire-breathers, including Vyr, who was even more terrifying than Damon.

"That's the last I've heard of him, too. He's in hiding again, but I need him soon."

"You mean you need his fire?"

Damon's jaw twitched as he clenched his teeth. He didn't answer that question, though. Instead, he gestured to Beaston and explained, "Things are going to get bad."

Jathan slid a glance to Beaston, then back to the keeper of these mountains. "Is this about Lynn?"

Beaston sat on the edge of Damon's desk. He looked exhausted in this lighting, like he hadn't slept in a week. "I see two things. Over and over. My son, Weston, sees two things. Over and over."

"The same things as you?"

Beaston nodded once.

Sheeeeyit. Jathan took a seat then, rested his elbows on his knees, and leaned forward. "What visions?"

"In the first, Lynn gets her way. You're standing over her. You're angry. Crying. Body shaking. Claw marks all over you. Bleeding out, but you don't care because the monster is lying on the ground staring at you. She has an 'I'm sorry' look right at the end. It's raining. Muddy. She tried and failed. You tried and failed."

Chills blasted against Jathan's skin, and he shook his head in denial. "I'll be damned if I let it happen."

"Good. You need that fight. So does she."

"Tell him the second vision, Beaston," Damon murmured.

"Second vision. The crew of two wars. Red Havoc won the first with dragon's fire and the son of Kong. It was close. The second war has two parts. War within Lynn, and war from the outside. Red Havoc is being hunted. New alpha, new ranks, and the panthers are scrambling to get their feet on the ground before they're hit."

"When?"

"Soon. Jathan, everyone is born with a destiny. Lynn's was big before she got broken. I've always been proud of her. She started out small and unwanted, and she got big. On-her-insides big. She has the biggest destiny maybe I've seen in a long time. She was born to be the storm, but something changed, and she went to her knees." Beaston licked his lips, and his green eyes churned like fire as he murmured, "Red Havoc's survival depends on Lynn's strength. Make her strong again. Make her the storm. Make her save them. Second vision. You're standing over her. You're proud. Body shaking. Claw marks all over you, bleeding. But you don't care because Monster is lying on the ground with her teeth on the neck of another monster. Lynn looks fierce, how I saw her before she quit fighting. It's raining. Blood is running in rivers, but she tried and succeeded." Beaston inhaled, his shoulders lifting with the breath. "In the second vision...*you* tried and succeeded."

Beaston arched his dark eyebrow and canted his head like an animal. "Be her spine. Keep her upright. Take her home."

EIGHT

A part of her wanted to go home.

Lynn clenched the pocket knife she'd found on her doorstep the day she moved into the treehouse. It was old and worn, and someone had engraved JB + LM. She had wondered at the owner, but didn't look a gift horse in the mouth. Swallowing the bile that crept up her throat, she opened the blade and etched a new mark into the wall. Five days left.

Before, she'd been ready, but now she wasn't so certain.

Carefully, she folded the blade into the

scuffed handle and shoved it in her back pocket. Her body hurt so bad she couldn't see straight. Hell, she hadn't wanted to fight earlier, but Monster took over her body and made her. Harrison hadn't wanted to answer her challenge, and then when it was through, Monster had laid there for an hour, waiting for Jathan to come and clutch her to his chest and carry her to the tree house. She'd become accustomed to that daily touch. Lynn just hadn't realized it until now. Today's fight had been one hundred percent about Monster wanting to be held by Jathan.

But he hadn't come, and then something awful had happened. Alone in the woods, she'd Changed back and forth uncontrollably for half an hour before she settled into her human skin and held. It hurt. It still hurt. She hated this. Human Lynn thought about what ifs. What if she could get control of Monster, what if she could try harder, what if she could be less tired, what if she could make it through the bad and eventually be okay? What if she could keep Jathan? What if she could keep Red Havoc? What if she could keep...she could keep...could keep...keep...Amberlynn?

The pain in her stomach at thinking her baby's name doubled her over. She'd tried so hard to let Amberlynn go because her life was better without Monster. Her baby could grow up and be a normal, beautiful, perfect panther-girl, raised by people who loved her, in the shadow and safety of Damon's Mountains. Mom and Dad could give her a better life than Lynn could. Lynn had known it was the right decision to give Amberlynn to her parents when she started going vacant. One time, she had woken up to Amberlynn crying, screaming, hungry, and Lynn hadn't known where she'd disappeared to while her baby needed her. One time, and she knew she loved her daughter too much to put her at risk like that. She loved her more than anything, much more than herself. Amberlynn was the greatest thing she'd ever done. She was proud of her. But giving her to her parents did something irreparable to her. She'd done the right thing by her daughter, kept her safe, but it had broken her the rest of the way.

Pocket knife heavy in her jeans, she grabbed a thin sweater and made her way out the door and down the stairs of the treehouse. She was restless, needed to move so her twitching muscles would get more blood flow to them and heal faster. It wasn't until she was standing in front of the Grayland Mobile Park sign that she realized she'd been walking through the woods with a purpose, and that purpose was a cute boy who had shown her more kindness and patience than anyone she'd ever met.

She made her way through the quiet trailer park, up the road to a long singlewide with giant weeds in the landscaping. She smiled at Henry— smiled! Jathan's truck wasn't parked in the yard, and the lights were off inside, so he still must've been working up at the Gray Backs' landing. Admittedly, she found it really sexy that he was a logger. It was hard, sweaty, muscle-rippling work. The fact that Jathan was a hard worker was extremely attractive because once upon a nightmare, she'd been with a man who hadn't been. Brody...fuck. She hunched over the pain in her middle, the pain of Monster asking for a Change. Lynn closed her eyes tightly and gritted out, "No." And then she forced herself to think of Brody. Her first mate had been lazy. He hadn't wanted to work. Even when she got pregnant, he'd refused to get a job, made her work extra hours on her feet all day, waiting tables so she could cover their bills. She'd ignored way too many red flags with him. Jathan, though, worked steadily and even admitted he hated the days he didn't get to work. Sure, that was because his bear was hard to manage, but still, he would never be a man who asked her to pay his bills.

The pain lessened, and she tried the name out in her mind again. *Brody*. The ache returned, but she didn't need to bend over to cope this time. *Brody, Brody, Brody, fuck-face-rat-bastard-dingleberry-lovin'-fart-footed-slimy-clam-turd*

Brody. Well okay, that had actually made her feel better.

Henry looked a little wilted and thirsty, so Lynn tramped through the fancy landscaping behind him to reach the water hose. After turning it on, she watered Henry and then the other giant weeds, and last of all, the perfectly manicured shrubs. She used to like gardening. She would make a vegetable garden behind her cabin every year, but somewhere along the way, she'd stopped doing that. Why had she stopped? All those hours working in the dirt had always been good for her.

For lack of anything to do, Lynn knelt down and plucked a tiny weed from under the branch of a shrub. And then another, and before she knew it, she was beautifying the landscaping further, careful to avoid the big weeds Jathan apparently kept as pets.

"You look really pretty right now," Jathan said from behind her.

Lynn startled hard because she hadn't heard

him approach. She spun and stood as fast as she could, feeling like she'd been caught doing something bad. Dirt sprinkled the grass as she dusted off her knees. "Sorry, I was just…"

Jathan stood strong and tall in the yard, his truck behind him, the sun setting behind the mountains. He was the pretty one, if a giant of a man covered in tattoos and reeking of dominance could be called pretty. He hadn't shaved this morning either, and his beard was thicker, but it didn't hide his slight smile. "Finish that thought. What are you doing? You aren't going to get in trouble with me."

"I went walking and ended up here," she rushed out. Lynn shrugged, and heat flooded her cheeks. "I watered Henry."

His smile stretched bigger and reached his dark eyes as he looked behind her at Henry. "You want to take care of him every day? He's at the end of his life and gets dried out during the day when I'm working. You could make him live longer if you give him water before I get home."

"Really? Ummm. Yeah, I can do that." For the next five days.

"Date number two."

"A yummy dinner and a movie?"

"You wish. Nope," he murmured approaching. "Tonight I'm going to seduce you with inedible tacos and forty-seven dick jokes told by my mother."

Lynn giggled. "Aren't I the lucky one?"

"Yes, because unbeknownst to my Ma, I'm going to text you filthy things all night, rev you up, touch your leg under the table, and when we get back tonight, I'm gonna wreck you."

His words had just made her go dumb, and now her mouth was hanging open. "Wreck...me?"

Jathan slid his hands to her waist and nodded, and now his smile had turned wicked. "I'm gonna wreck you so good you'll quit putting those fucking marks on your wall just to stay here and warm my bed, waiting for me to take care of you." Jathan arched his eyebrows and dragged her waist against his. "And I *will* take care of you, Lynn."

"I like when you call me that," she whispered drunkenly.

The smile slipped from his face. "You don't like the pet names?"

"Everyone calls me pet names. They call me Crazy Lynn. I like that you are the only one who calls me just Lynn."

While he dragged a fingertip down her cheek, he watched his touch with a troubled look in his eyes. "You aren't crazy. You're just tired."

"And weak."

"Not true. Brody left you a year ago, and where are you?"

"Here, at the end of my life like Henry. All dried up. You're watering me to prolong it."

"Stop. A year buckled under Monster, and you're still alive. You're exhausted, Lynn. You tried to do this on your own, and it didn't work. You got tired, not weak. You needed someone under your arm, dragging you when your legs went numb." He tipped his head to the side.

"That's me now."

"You gonna drag me through life? Sounds pretty unfair to you."

"Doesn't feel unfair. Feels like the most important thing I've ever done. You know you're worth the effort, right? You know you're valuable? You are to me."

She felt unsettled with his easy declarations. "I don't understand you."

"What don't you understand? I say what I mean, say how I feel. You can hear the honest notes in my voice. I'm upfront, no games."

"You're different than I remember."

"What do you remember?"

Lynn scrunched up her face and concentrated. "My thoughts get muddy. I don't think about when I used to live here much anymore. I remember you were a ladies man and a bad boy. You drove a motorcycle to school and gave the pretty girls rides after the last bell. You were funny with your brother, but with everyone else, you were quieter. Jax was always mouthy, but you watched more. I caught you watching me at lunch a lot, but you would always look away. I remember I built up the courage to talk to you twice. You left fast the first time, and you turned and talked to someone else the second. But one night, right before I left, I went to this party. And you were there."

God, she hadn't thought about this in so long it was like seeing the memory through murky pond water. "I came out of the bathroom upstairs, and you were there, leaning against the wall, on your phone, looking bored. I tripped on the edge of a rug in the hallway, and you caught me. You touched me, and I felt this...electricity. It hurt so I flinched away, and so did you. We stood there looking at each other. You looked upset, your eyes were turning green, and people were walking all around us. Humans." She closed her eyes so she could see the memory better. "You smelled like fur, you were shaking, and I wanted to fix it. I wanted to make you feel better, so I rested my hands on your chest and told you, 'I'm here.' And you leaned down and kissed me. I'd already liked you for a while, so my body reacted. I pressed against you and kissed you back. It was perfect, touching you like I wanted to. Like the pretty girls got to touch you. I was happy. I felt like I wasn't on the outside for once. I *belonged* for this incredible moment in time. Everything was perfect. And then you pushed me back gently and told me… Do you remember?"

When she opened her eyes, Jathan no longer faced her. He was staring off in the woods and looked like he wanted to retch. "Yeah. I told you the same thing I told everyone who got too close to me. I said, 'I don't want you.' It's a huge regret. I didn't know about you being given up for adoption, or that you were trying to get your foster parents to adopt you. I didn't know you always felt unwanted until later when I told Jax about it, and he beat the shit out of me for being a dick. It was one of the biggest fights we ever got into, and I deserved the bleeding he gave me. You never talked to me again. You disappeared.

When my crew had that party the day you got adopted? I went behind Creed's trailer with a bottle of Jameson and drank myself to oblivion. You carry big guilt, Lynn." Jathan pulled her against him and rested his chin on top of her head. "So do I."

"Wait…" She eased back and looked up at him, discomfort swirling her heart. "You don't blame yourself for me leaving to find a crew…do you?"

"A little. I was a jerk to you, made you feel like I didn't want you, but it was bullshit. I thought you were so pretty, but you scared me. I don't believe in all that love crap." His brows lowered. "Or I didn't want to maybe. You were making me feel things that scared me. They were changing who I was, what I believed in, and what I didn't believe in. And that kiss? It fucked with my head. It settled my bear instantly. I was on fire, ready for a Change, and you controlled my animal like you were a damn beast whisperer. I didn't want anyone to have that control over me but me. You felt dangerous—"

"Me? I felt dangerous?" She shoved out of his arms and took three steps back to put some distance between them. "I'm a panther, no match for a bear shifter!"

"That's not what I mean," he said, approaching slow, his palms up like he was trying to calm a rabid animal.

The panther was snarling in her throat, but fuck it. She had a thought, and it was a terrifying thought, and the clearer it became, the more it hurt. "Is your guilt why you're being my friend now?"

Jathan halted and reared his head back like he'd been slapped. "What?"

"Is that why you're trying to save me? Because of what happened at some dumb party when we were kids? I left because I wanted to leave, Jathan. No one had anything to do with me ending up in Red Havoc, and I don't regret it. I loved my crew! I love them still! I'll always... Fuck." She sobbed and dragged in a deep breath.

"Sin number two, you ready?"

"It won't scare me off," Jathan growled out. "I know that's what you're doing. I can see the running in your eyes, and you'll tell me something awful to try and make me run because you really think I'm here out of some sense of guilt, not because I care about you. The real you. The one you hide from the world, but not from me. Shock me, Lynn. Watch me stand here. I won't give you my back, that's a promise, so fucking do it. Cut yourself with your guilt in front of me. Make me watch. I'm ready. You're ready. Do it. Do it now."

"When Brody got me pregnant, I had never been happier. I was with Red Havoc, and I adored them. I belonged. Brody made me feel like he was mine and that we were bonded, and then I was going to have a cub. I was going to be the best mom, the best parent for this little cub. And then I found text messages in Brody's phone to Winter, who had moved to a different crew. She never responded, but his texts to her were desperate to get her back. There were tons of them. I was so angry and felt so betrayed that I pushed him out. I kicked him out of our cabin. I went on tirades. I hated him. I was so mad because I'd lost Winter for him. I'd betrayed my friend for him, and we weren't just mated, Jathan. We got married too, after we found out we were pregnant, and he tried to go back to her the week of our wedding. I was never enough. So okay, I was going to raise this little cub by myself. I fell apart for a little while, but I was still working, still earning money, still trying... I was going to be the best single parent for my cub. But the bond I'd formed with Brody was hurting me. When he left the crew, there was this huge hole in my chest, like I'd been hit straight through with a cannonball and was walking around trying to pretend I was still alive and everything was fine. And then when he was out there in the world, he was going crazy right along with me. I could tell from the messages he left. I wouldn't pick up the phone, because I was so determined to be strong and have some pride in myself. He was spiraling, and his messages made less and less sense, and eventually, he would just growl into the phone, like his panther was in control. He was my poison, because I was falling apart without him, and I was his poison because he went crazy and did awful things. He hurt people. Changed people against their will. Ben says that innocent blood is on his hands, but it never was. It's on mine. Those people got hurt because I wasn't enough. When I found out he was killed, the hole took over my entire body. The only thing that kept me going was the swell of my stomach. It was every tiny kick, every movement. I was clinging to Amberlynn for survival before she was even born." The cannonball was back just talking about this. "I can't do this." The edge of her vision was going dark. Panicked, Lynn went to her knees in the dirt and gripped her hair, screamed in agony.

"Finish it." Jathan was standing right in front of her. "Do it fast."

She stared at the crisscrossed scuffs on his work boots as she choked out, "And then I had her, and she was perfect, but I was going to ruin her because I couldn't stay present anymore. I didn't trust my panther around her. She was tiny and needed me, and I was in the tree house because I couldn't be around the crew anymore. I was scared for her. I was scared of Monster. So I quit."

"That's bullshit. You didn't quit. You kept her safe."

"I gave her to my parents. It was supposed to be temporary. A week. Maybe two so I could get ahold of myself and get better— be better for her. So I could be the mom I wanted to be. But I just got worse and worse, and weeks turned to months. I would call my mom, and Amberlynn would be gurgling in the background. She was never crying when I called. She was safe and happy, but I am selfish, Jathan. I'm so fucking selfish because I still considered taking her back even when I was falling apart. I wanted to be the one feeding her, holding her, singing her lullabies, giving her baths, and watching her firsts. I was missing everything. This is the person you are trying to save. Someone who would give up their child."

"Lynn, you think you're the only one who gave up a baby? Do you really?" Jathan knelt down and gripped her shoulders. "Look at me." He shook her gently. "Lynn, look at me."

Her heart breaking, she dragged her gaze to his. Jathan was all beautiful shadows, and she tried hard to hold on, gripping his wrists to anchor herself in the moment.

"Don't disappear until you hear me. You made a sacrifice. You sacrificed yourself for your daughter. You did. You are a good mom because you made sure she was safe. You put your pride aside so she could have a good life. Of course, you wanted her back. That doesn't make you selfish. That makes you a mother with instincts. I've seen her. Lynn!" Jathan shook her gently. "Medusa! Stay with me, Lynn. Did you hear me? I said I've seen her. I've seen Amberlynn."

Hold on! Lynn curled over the pain in her middle but kept her eyes locked on Jathan's. "You have?"

"Yeah, I've been visiting her every few days since you came back from Red Havoc. I wanted to understand you, so I went to your parents, and she was there, holding onto the coffee table, wearing this cute little pink tutu with ladybugs on it. Her eyes stay gold. Her hair is bright red like yours. She looks just like you, except she smiles all the time like you used to. She's happy because you made a hard decision for her."

Lynn's shoulders shook with her sobbing, and she barely got out, "Did you hold her?"

Jathan nodded. "Once. She pulled up on the couch I was sitting on. She was using my knee for balance. She's so fucking close to walking, Lynn. She reached for me so I picked her up. She smelled like a little panther. Fur. Smiles. She'll be a little badass, just like you."

"I'm not a badass," Lynn whispered.

"No? You just talked about Amberlynn, and where are you?"

Chest heaving, Lynn looked around at the retreating shadows.

"Are you still here with me?" Jathan asked low.

Lynn wiped her damp cheeks with the back of her hand and sat up straighter. Monster was quiet in her middle. "Yeah, I'm still here with you."

And a tiny piece of her, for the first time in a long time, felt like the beginnings of a badass.

NINE

There was muffled yelling inside of Willa and Matt Barns' singlewide trailer in the Grayland Mobile Park. Willa was upset about something. Lynn hesitated on knocking and gave Jathan a questioning glance over her shoulder.

"Ma might be a little weirder than usual tonight," Jathan murmured.

Lynn frowned. "I feel like it's impossible for Willa to be any weirder."

Jathan snorted and wrapped his hand around Lynn's. It was big and strong and covered hers completely. "I already ordered real tacos too, because Ma is the worst at making them. It's like she tries to suck." He pushed open the door and barged in.

"That can't be true—" When the smell of sauerkraut and taco seasoning hit her nose, Lynn nearly gagged.

"Furthermore," Willa yelled, "I'll fight all of them. Every single one! Take my worms? I'd like to see them try it!"

Jathan turned to Lynn and snickered silently.

What did you do? she mouthed.

Jathan only winked and pulled her into the living room by the hand. "Ma, I'd like you to meet Lynn."

"Dumbass, I already know her."

"I know, I just wanted to annoy you. Smells horrible in here."

"Boy, tonight isn't the night to sass my tacos." Willa held up a handful of letters. There was a huge pile of them on the kitchen table. "Some idiot has formed a group called WANKE. War Against Nerds Killing Earthworms. I thought it had to be some mistake until the government cease and desist letters started arriving this afternoon. And there are three assholes picketing the entrance to Damon's Mountains, and there was yellow caution tape around my entire worm house today like it was a crime scene! They're going to take my worms!"

Jathan made his way over to a bowl of cherries on the counter and shrugged. "Maybe you could start up a different business."

Willa's mouth plopped open, and the letters fell from her hands like a shower in a rainforest.

Jathan's giant father, Matt, was leaned back in a chair in the kitchen, staring at his son with narrowed eyes and the smallest quirk to his lips, as if he smelled a rat.

In a shaky voice, Willa whispered, "What else could I possibly do that would bring me as much joy as worms?"

Jathan bit a cherry in half and leveled his mother with a dead-eyed look. "Maybe you could be a dick knitter."

Willa froze, and her eyes blazed bright green. Three seconds passed before she gritted out, "Boy, you tell me right now if this was your doing."

Jathan gave her a carefree smile as he smacked loudly on his cherry.

Matt snorted, but pursed his lips against a laugh and wouldn't meet Willa's glare when it arched to him. She looked down at the letters on the floor and then to the mountain of letters on the table. She sounded utterly shocked as she murmured, "I just rampaged for three straight hours."

When Jathan's smile got bigger, Lynn had to bite her bottom lip to hide her grin.

Louder, Willa repeated, "I just rampaged for three straight hours, Jathan!"

"Well you should stop knitting dicks and putting them in my house! Dick coasters, dick throw rugs, a dick blanket, dick napkins, dick hand towels... Ma! You knitted me dick shoes and hid my work boots! I tried them on. You made them too small, and my big toes hung out of the pee-pee holes."

"I just started the dick prank last week. This!" She yanked up a handful of letters, her straight red hair twitching in its ponytail. "This took weeks of premeditated planning!"

Matt full-on covered his smile with his hand.

Willa looked from face to face. Her bottom lip quivered, and her bright green eyes rimmed with moisture.

Well, that broke Lynn's heart, so she stepped forward to give Willa a hug, but Jathan stopped her. "Wait for it," he muttered, staring at his mom.

"I'm really proud of you," Willa said in an emotional voice.

Matt barked a laugh and cleared his throat to cover it. Jathan was chuckling too as he made his way to Willa and pulled her into a hug. "I knew you would be, Ma. Now stop making these shitty tacos. I've ordered us tacos. You want me to throw all the letters away?"

"No," Willa said, hugging her son tight. "I want to keep them with your school stuff and trophies. Who did all this?"

"Uuuh, every crew I could get ahold of, and I made the government stamp with a piece of rubber. I really wanted the group to be called WANKER, but I couldn't figure out any words that made sense and started with an R. I paid three townies forty bucks each to stand out there and picket when you came home. I was the one who put the caution tape on the worm house. Also, seriously...please stop decorating my house with dicks."

"Okay," Willa said in a tiny voice, "I'll knit you vaginas next time instead."

"That's all I ask," Jathan murmured, patting his mom gently on the back.

God, this was the weirdest family. Lynn stood there with a big dumb grin on her face. She loved them.

Willa sniffed and shoved Jathan away. "Remember I gave you life, boy, and I can take it away. No pranks with my worms ever again. That's sacred."

Jathan's phone rang with the Baby Got Back song as his ringtone. "Yeah?" he answered. "Okay, I'll be right there." He hung up and shoved his cell in his back pocket, then told them, "The food is here, but the guy is afraid to cross into Damon's Mountains to deliver. I'm gonna meet him at the main road."

"Okay," Willa said in a distracted voice as she sifted through letters one by one on the table.

Jathan looked down at Lynn and parted his lips to say something, but Matt interrupted. "I'll come with you." He pushed between them, yanked the front door open, then looked back impatiently at his son.

Jathan gave his dad a what-the-fuck look, and then he did something that shocked Lynn to her bones. He turned to her and dragged her waist close, and then he leaned down and brushed his lips against hers. It happened so fast she didn't even have time to react. He kissed her, and then

he squeezed her hips once, dumping warmth
into her middle in an instant. He released her
and left without another word or a single look
back.

Lynn touched her lips with her fingertips and
watched the door close behind him.

Holy. Shit. She really liked when he touched
her and when he was affectionate. She'd thought
she wouldn't ever want that with a man again.
After Brody, she'd deemed men unreliable,
untrustworthy, soul-sucking creatures who
should be avoided. But Jathan was different. He
felt different. He was dangerous, a Bad Bear, a
commitment-phobe from birth, and he'd been in
trouble since he was a cub. So why did the most
dangerous man she could possibly choose...also
feel like the safest?

"Jathan has never brought a girl home," Willa
said.

With a slow blink, Lynn ripped her gaze away
from the door and looked at Willa. Her eyes were
still green and her head was canted like an

animal.

Lynn asked, "Really?"

"I would be happy for him, but you have checked out, haven't you, little kitty? You've quit? You're counting down the days until Creed tells Benson Saber you can't be saved...aren't you?"

Chest heaving and head swirling with confusion, Lynn nodded slightly. That was the plan. Before Jathan.

"Surely you can see why his father and I aren't excited about the prospect of our son getting attached to someone who will disappear. We never worried about Jaxon. He was a rogue, but he attached to friends here. Jathan never attached to anyone. He kept himself distant on purpose. Maybe it's his animal, or maybe it's just how he is as a man. But I just watched my boy, who I thought would never pick a girl, kiss you. And from the look on your face, you liked it. You're encouraging him."

Anger pulsed through her at being reprimanded by Willa. "I'm not meaning for this to happen," Lynn growled low.

"Then stop it."

"I can't."

"Then stick around."

"I. Can't."

Willa slammed her open palm on the table so hard the legs screeched across the wooden floor an inch. "Do you realize who you will hurt when you leave? You will cut him, Lynn. You have a daughter too—"

"Stop it."

"You have a daughter, and do you know how fucking bad I want her?"

"What?" Lynn asked, confused as she backed toward the front door to bolt. No, no, no, she couldn't talk about this again. Not when she was already emotionally drained.

"I want a granddaughter. I want to spoil Amberlynn. I want to watch my son hold her, and I want to see the kind of dad he could be—"

"She isn't mine!"

"And she never will be if you quit now! Don't

you take that easy way out, Lynn. You fucking fight. I know you're tired. I know you are. I can smell how exhausted and sick in the head you are. I can feel it. It makes my bear want to fight. It makes everyone around here want to fight. You think you're the only one with a problem animal? Beaston put a bear in me without my consent. And not just a bear, a damn alpha. One who is hard to manage on a good day. I want to fight Creed all the time. I want to Change all the time, but do you know what I am?"

Lynn's face crumpled as her shoulder blades hit the door. "No," she whispered.

Willa's lip snarled up. "I'm a fighter. And do you know what you are?"

"Not a fighter," Lynn whispered.

"Wrong. You have anchors now that you aren't paying attention to. Jathan is building a bond. Can't you feel it? I can practically see it. If you go, you'll destroy him, and he'll never pick another. If you go, Amberlynn will suffer. If you go, I'll never have the daughter of my heart that I wanted for my son. You'll hurt all of us, and you leaving, even if it's easy on you, will echo through these mountains and Red Havoc mountains for a lifetime. I'm ready for my battle now."

"W-what?"

"My turn. You've been working your way through everyone, right? Seeing who you think you can get to lose control on you and end it? I'll fucking do it. Give me that kill shot, Lynn. Give me your neck, and I'll break it. I'll put you out of your misery, but remember what you stand to lose." Willa jammed her finger at the front door. "Outside. Now."

"I—I don't understand."

"Tonight, right now, you'll choose to live or die, and you'll stick with that decision. Get. Out. Side."

Lynn's panther snarled inside of her, and her vision blurred. Everything was tinted in red. Red Willa, red hair, red face, red eyes. Monster was clawing at her skin. Finally...a real fight.

"No, I'm not ready," Lynn whispered to the

cat. But her hand reached for the door, and her feet moved jerkily forward until she was on the porch, on the stairs, and then in the front yard.

When she reached the center of the clearing, the popping of bones sounded behind her, and then a challenging roar bellowed out so loud, it shook the earth beneath her feet.

Lynn trembled with terror as her body buckled. Monster wanted this. She was ready.

But I'm not.

Jathan…Amberlynn…Willa…Matt…Red Havoc…her bird…*my bird*! Her best friend, Eden, would be so sad after tonight. Lynn would always be a disappointment to everyone. Jathan, Jathan, Jathan. He could stop this if he was here. There were glowing eyes all around them. The Gray Backs were gathering to watch her end. Beaston was there with a raven on his arm. He looked so sad. He looked as sad as Lynn had felt for the last year, when she'd housed more ghosts than a damn graveyard. Pain blasted through her as the Change destroyed her human body and transformed her into Monster. All four paws hit the earth, and she spun to the sound of the charging grizzly. Willa's green eyes glowed with determination. She really would end this. *Fuck. Jathan! I'm not ready, I'm not ready. Jathan!*

Her body wasn't her own. Monster controlled her as she ran for the grizzly and slammed into her chest. Time slowed.

There was pain. Lynn fought like hell to hide her neck, but she took a claw to the back as she sank her teeth into Willa's shoulder. She closed her eyes to chomp down harder, and when she opened them, she could see him. Her Jathan. Matt and Creed were holding him back. He was yelling. Furious Bad Bear. Mad at her. Willa would end her, and he would never forgive his mom. He would never hug her so gently like he had in the house, and it would be all Lynn's fault for not being strong enough.

Fuck. That.

Pain, pain, pain. She was protecting herself, playing defense, but it was hard. Monster was prepping for her signature move—the one where she hurt the predator just enough to get them angry, and then she gave them her neck. *No! Jathan, help!*

She was slammed to the ground, her teeth ripping through Willa's skin. The massive brown bear had death in her eyes as she lifted her paw with six-inch curved claws into the air. Monster jerked her head to the side. Victory.

No, fuck Monster's victory. Lynn closed her eyes and tried with every ounce of strength to protect her vitals. Willa slammed her paws on either side of her and roared a death warning. When Monster exposed her neck again, Lynn could see the hurt in Jathan's eyes. One split second in witnessing that pain, and everything Willa had said flashed through her mind. She was going to hurt a man who had been kind to her. Who had tried to make her stronger.

Lynn roared and forced her body to move so that Willa's paw missed, and hit her on the side instead of the neck. Oh, it hurt, but she was still breathing. Still screaming. And with the most effort she'd ever given, Lynn battled Monster for her body. She tucked that fucking panther into her skin until her roar was a hoarse, human scream.

On her knees, naked and shaking, bleeding, chest heaving, fists clenched. Lynn lifted her infuriated gaze to Willa and said, "I'm. Not. Ready."

Willa lifted her giant block head high and looked down her snout at her, lips curled back, eyes blazing and narrowed. For a second, Lynn thought it was anger etched on the grizzly's face, but when Willa began to back away slowly, her expression morphed to one of respect. *Good girl*, she seemed to say.

Everything hurt, and Lynn couldn't drag in a breath. She sat there panting for the span of three blinks, and then she rose up and made her way past Creed toward the woods. She was going to fall apart, and she didn't want anyone to see this.

That had been her chance. That had been her fucking chance, but Jathan was in her head, and so was Willa, and she hated it here. Hated everything. Feeling hurt. It hurt! And everyone here was so damn determined for her to feel this stuff she'd been trying to suppress for all this time.

The second the first tear hit the pine needles, Lynn bolted. She ran like demons were chasing her, and maybe they were. Her demons. They'd tried to eat her alive but failed, and now she was caught in the in-between. Life and death, except the life part was pretend. She hadn't been living for a long time. She'd been walking this earth a ghost, and now too many people were trying to do the impossible. They were trying to revive her.

"Lynn, stop!" Jathan yelled as his hand ripped her arm back. He spun her and gripped her shoulders when she balked.

"Not everyone is redeemable!" she screamed.

"You're wrong! You're wrong about you,

Lynn."

She jerked out of his grasp, gripped her hair and screamed in agony as she tried to keep her body. Monster wanted to go back for Willa. With a sob, she turned away from Jathan and made her way across a deer trail. Brush and thorns scraped her bare legs, but she didn't care. She shook so bad, every muscle in her body was twitching, but it wasn't from the cold. She was in a war to keep her body. She was in a war for Jathan, and he didn't even know it.

He grabbed her from behind and wrapped his arms around her. In her ear, between her agonized screams, he said, "Bond to me. Let it happen. I'm not Brody. I'm telling you right now...listen to my voice...listen for lies, and you'll find none. I'm yours. I'm not going anywhere. Do what you have to do, Lynn. Fucking break. I'll watch after you, watch you fall apart, and I'll be right here to put you back together again."

"Sin number three," she sobbed, sagging in his arms.

"Tell me."

"I took Barret into a war with the lions because I was scared to die alone. I couldn't think straight at the end of my time with Red Havoc. I couldn't keep my panther from Changing. My body hurt so bad, and he was broken, too. In some fucked-up corner of my mind, I thought it would be easier on both of us if we just went to war and disappeared." Lynn turned and hugged Jathan as hard as she could. "I almost got one of my friends killed because I wasn't strong enough to think straight. Do you still think I'm redeemable?"

Jathan let off a long sigh and stroked her hair back from her face. He cupped her cheeks, lifted her gaze to his, and searched her eyes. "Yes."

That one word shattered what she thought of the world. It shattered her bitterness like mirror glass under a sledge hammer. *Yes.* One person thought she was redeemable when she didn't see it in herself, and it made all the difference.

"Love is fire," she whispered.

"Yes," Jathan murmured.

"Love can burn you to the ground."

"Yes. And now it's time to get up out of the ashes. I'll tell you something. Something vulnerable like you're doing with me. I've always loved watching fragile things break. I thought anything fragile deserved to be broken. Glass shattering was my favorite sound in the world. Now I'll hate it. There is nothing worse than watching something break. You've ruined everything, Lynn. Maybe I was the weak one all along, because look at me now. Big Bad Bear begging something fragile not to shatter, or I'll shatter right along with you."

"I don't want that. I want to protect you."

He winced like it hurt him to admit. "Same. You scared me tonight. I watched you give my mom your neck, watched you fight it, then give it again, over and over, and I didn't want to let you go. Tell me how you got here, Lynn. To this moment, here in the woods, with me."

She waited for her vision to cloud and for her

panther to scratch at her skin, but neither happened. She'd been hiding the dark parts of herself from the world for so long, it was terrifying to trust someone with it all. But...Jathan saw her—really *saw* her—and he hadn't run.

Fucking break. I'll watch after you, watch you fall apart, and I'll be right here to put you back together again.

He'd dared her to show him her worst, and then he promised to lock his legs against Hurricane Lynn. She'd thought no one on Earth would've been strong enough, but Jathan was.

And so she trusted him. "With every decision I made, whether it was a bad one or a good one that went wrong, this hole inside of me grew and grew until I was just...emptiness. And one day I woke up and I wasn't standing anymore. Maybe I hadn't been for a long time. Maybe I had always been on my knees and hadn't realized it." Lynn swallowed hard and gripped the fabric of his T-shirt, right over his hips. And then she admitted the most terrifying combination of words that had ever come from her lips because she could really fail badly at this and let him down. "I want to learn how to stand again."

Slowly, the corners of Jathan's lips curved up with pride. "I think you just did."

Her throat hurt from screaming, her head hurt from fighting Monster, and every muscle in her body ached. She was shaking and cold, like her body still couldn't regulate its temperature well. She had damp cheeks, and her hair flew wildly around her face. She probably looked like hell, but Jathan was moving in closer and brushing his fingertips down her arm softly, lifting gooseflesh from her skin where he touched her. And when he pulled her waist against his, she could feel it. His erection pressed against her belly.

He turned her slightly and winced at the long claw marks that curved from her ribs to her hip. She didn't like when he worried over nothing.

"If I don't look, I can make it not hurt."

His gaze twitched to hers, and his soft brown eyes stirred with concern. "How?"

Uncomfortable, she shrugged up one shoulder. "Somewhere along the way, I wanted to stop feeling the hurt. I've fought so much I can just put the pain away where it doesn't touch me. I can flip a switch and not feel anymore." Or maybe she was already partly dead. Where that thought would've made her feel relief before, now it only made her feel sick. She didn't want to be dead anymore.

He ran his fingertip softly down the side of one of her healing claw marks. "I hope you know how beautiful you are."

"Me?" she asked.

Jathan gave her a wicked grin and pulled her hand to his jeans, pressed it against his bulging erection.

Equal parts elated and baffled, she asked, "You want me like this? Like a mess?"

He leaned down and kissed her fast, sucked her lip hard, and then released her. He nodded. "I don't mind your mess. It was sexy as fuck watching you stand up just now, little monster. What a hellion you'll be when you get through this. You realize no one has fight experience like you do...right? You just went after a mother-fucking grizzly shifter, Second in the Gray Back Crew, and you held your own. And you fought to live. No more counting down days, Lynn. You're stuck here with me. I saw that fight in your eyes tonight so yeah, I want to give you another anchor."

"What anchor?" she whispered.

Jathan slid his hand between her legs and pushed his finger inside of her until she gasped at how good it felt.

He rubbed his cheek against hers, rough beard against her soft skin, until his lips brushed her earlobe. "Me."

"You're bribing me to stay here with sex?"

Jathan chuckled. "Not just sex, Lynn. Not a one night stand. I'm gonna get you addicted to me. You won't ever want to go."

"Can I tell you a secret?" She needed to do it quick because he was pushing his finger into her in a slow rhythm that had her rocking against his hand and clutching onto his shirt.

"You can tell me anything." The conviction in his voice made her smile. She really could, and he wouldn't run. There was triumph in that.

"I already don't want to go," she admitted softly.

A rumble sounded from his chest. He pulled his shirt over his head and pressed it to the claw marks on her ribs, and then he backed her toward a clearing between the pines. When his right foot moved forward, her left moved back at the same time, gracefully, smoothly, keeping the same distance between them as he guided her backward. She didn't get nervous about tripping on something, because she trusted him. He would catch her before she fell. That's just how Jathan was with her. When she was the faller, he was the catcher. Their movement through the woods was like a dance. Her body reacted and countered his as if they'd moved like this a hundred times before.

The intensity of his eyes burned right through her as he murmured, "Every time I imagined what it would be like to be with you, I wanted to take you rough. I wanted to fuck you. I wanted to own you. I wanted to take you fast and hard, until you screamed my name."

"And now?"

"Now I want to ruin you for any other man. I want tonight to be all you crave. When you touch yourself from here on, I want you to only think about me. I want you addicted to my touch. Addicted to me."

She reached for his jeans and hooked her fingers in the waist. And then she slid them inward, brushing the top of his swollen shaft. Jathan stopped stalking her and softly dragged his fingers down her neck, then cupped it and kissed her. It was slow sips that melted her, calmed her twitching, aching muscles. It was a strange feeling, having someone else have such an impact on her body. This is what Jathan was talking about at that party all those years ago. This is what had scared him—having someone else affect him so deeply. It was the loss of control to someone who could crush her heart with a squeeze of his hand. How terrifying and exhilarating to trust him with her heart after all she'd been through.

She unfastened his jeans as he angled her head back to suck on her neck. When his teeth scraped her skin, she swayed forward against him with a tiny, needy sound. He felt so good touching her. Intimidating man. Brave man. People called him Bad Bear but he was a good man. He was good for her. Good to her. He'd held her baby. He'd visited her parents to try to understand her better. He'd watched her all these weeks and made sure no one put her down. He'd been protecting her, and she was only just realizing how much.

Good Bear. My Bear.

He was sucking on her neck harder now and

she pushed his pants down by inches, unsheathing him. Jathan was a big man everywhere. His size was intimidating, but she knew he would be gentle until her body got used to him. That's the kind of man he was. Patient, caring, and put her needs first. Maybe he hadn't attached to other people, but he was really good at attaching to her. She didn't know why they worked, only that they did.

Inhaling deeply, he picked her up suddenly and held her tightly against him as she wrapped her legs around his waist. She closed her eyes. This was like flying. Being with him wasn't a cage like with Brody. Being with Jathan was freedom. Freedom from the ache in her heart, freedom from her demons, freedom from having time lost.

He didn't realize it yet...be he was already her anchor.

Lynn's stomach dipped, and then her back rested gently on the grass. Jathan's pants were still hanging halfway down his hips, but he shoved them down farther in one graceful motion.

When the head of his swollen cock slid into her by an inch, she tossed her head back and moaned. His body was silk and steel under her hands. Powerful chest, covered in tattoos, but smooth. When she ran her hands along his top two abs, he twitched and huffed a breath as though her touch was ecstasy. His arms were locked on either side of her face, triceps bulging, the epitome of power and dominance, but he was keeping his weight off her, keeping her comfortable. His hips rolled against her slowly as he pushed into her deeper. God, he was big, but perfect. No pain, just pleasure. Deeper, then deeper again, and finally he slid into her fully, filling and stretching her.

He lowered himself to his elbows, one hand gripping the back of her head as he pulled her close and kissed her, hips never pausing against hers. So slow. Beautiful agony since he'd created such a fire in her middle. Every thrust built this tingling sensation inside of her that she was desperate for more of. It had been so long since she felt like this. So long since she felt anything. So long. Fuuuuck, he was good. Faster now, so graceful, hitting her clit just right every time he buried himself inside of her. His muscles tensed. His kisses grew more urgent, tongue thrusting against hers in a rhythm with his hips. He bit her bottom lip, harder and harder, until she begged with little mewling sounds. *Fucking do it. Bite me.*

So close. The pressure was so intense her entire body was trembling with how good he felt inside her. He slowed again, three strokes, and then sped up, toying with her, building the heat between them. Jathan knew exactly how to touch her.

He let more of his weight rest on her but it wasn't uncomfortable. She felt safe. Safe? God, this was everything. Sooo close. Sooo deep. Lynn gripped the back of his hair once, then lost her mind and clawed him...just raked her nails down his back. He arched so beautifully and snarled, but he didn't flinch away. He slammed into her hard. More weight on her.

Scratch.

"Fuck," Jathan whispered in a shaky breath. "Again."

Scratch.

She nuzzled his bicep, testing him. Fast as she could, she turned her face and bit him lightly, right over a tapestry of geometric tattoos that covered most of his arm. He didn't run. He snarled up his lips in a devilish smile and dared her with his blazing green eyes.

"One," he counted, bucking into her deep.

He pulled out slowly and rested his lips where her neck and shoulder met. "Two," he murmured against her skin, slamming into her again.

"I'm there," she whispered desperately.

Another deep rumble sounded from him as he growled out, "Three."

And as he thrust into her hard, he bit down on her skin. She gasped at the pain of it, because this one did hurt. It wasn't like battle wounds.

She'd given her mind to this—to him. One second of pain, but then she was distracted by the orgasm that blasted through her. He didn't release her like she thought he would. He sustained the pain and the pleasure as he slammed into her faster and faster. And as his cock pulsed deep within her, she repaid him. She gripped the back of his arm and bit his bicep as hard as she could. She was lost in waves of ecstasy, barely able to think as she claimed him back. He was throbbing so deep within her, filling her up until warmth trickled out of her. His hand was tight on the back of her hair, and with his other, he yanked her knee up with a fierce grip and rolled his hips against her, slammed into her even deeper. She released her bite just so she could gasp his name as her release intensified. The pleasure consumed her, and she arched her back against the ground just to be closer to him. Just to feel his skin on hers.

Jathan eased back and just stared at her as their aftershocks pulsed on together, as their chests heaved and their claiming marks bled. She was completely and happily trapped in his gaze because the green had faded. He didn't look wild anymore. His soft brown eyes were filled with awe as he searched her face.

He gently stroked her hair back. "Stay," he demanded in a hoarse whisper. "Now you have to stay."

She was too full of emotion to answer without conjuring tears, so she stroked her knuckles against his short, dark beard and smiled. And then she made the first promise that she had in a long time. A promise she was determined to keep because Jathan had made life a little more beautiful.

Lynn nodded. She was going to stay.

For Jathan, because he deserved the effort.

For Amberlynn, because she deserved a strong mother.

For Red Havoc and the Gray Backs.

But most of all...

Lynn was going to stay for herself.

TEN

Lynn frowned at the letter taped to the door of Willa and Matt's singlewide. It was constructed of cut-out magazine letters that had been glued to a piece of computer paper. If she was confused about it being a ransom note before, the title *If you want your tacos, do what I say* across the top cleared that right up.

Scavenger hunt, my little woodland diddlers. I have stolen four beers from Creed and a flask of whiskey from Clinton at great risk to myself. Help me drink them. First stop, Beaston's Treehouse. Or as we were calling it lately, Crazy Lynn's treehouse. I don't think you're so crazy anymore, ya lil scrapper. Use the four-wheeler. It probably has gas in it. Put some pants on.

Green M&Ms, Orange M&Ms.

Jathan, don't fuck this up. Your girl needs some fun in her life.

Willawonka

Lynn finished reading first so she was able to see the curve of Jathan's smile.

He murmured, "Hell yes to this. You do need some fun." And then he folded up the paper, shoved it in his back pocket, and pulled her by the hand toward a four-wheeler that sat in the yard, right on the edge of the porch light.

"I haven't ridden one of these in a long time," she said, tugging at the hem of Jathan's oversize T-shirt she was wearing.

Jathan hopped on and started the ATV. Standing with his legs locked, he revved the engine and waggled his eyebrows. "Get on, and you get to play with my abs."

Lynn snorted. "Cocky boy."

"Cocky *man*." He sat down and said, "Now get on this thing before I drag you, caveman style."

Well okay, that was actually sexy. Lynn climbed on behind him and slid her arms around his waist, and then they were off. Like with his Harley, Jathan wasn't a slow driver on ATVs either. Lynn left her stomach somewhere back in the Grayland Mobile Park as he blasted up the mountain toward her treehouse. She hadn't even adjusted to the speed before they were there. Two canned beers sat on the bottom stair of the treehouse with a folded piece of paper fluttering in the breeze between them.

Excited, Lynn hopped off and bounded over to the next clue. She read it out loud. "Lynn, take this opportunity to put some pants on. Your hoohah is showing. The Barns men like granny panties best—

"We actually don't," Jathan argued. "I like lacy see-through thongs or nothing at all."

With a giggle, Lynn finished reading it. "Shotgun these and find your next drinks at the top of Bear Trap Falls." Lynn frowned up at Jathan. His smile was stunning as he watched her. "What's shotgunning?"

"You've never shotgunned a beer before?"

"Nope."

Jathan leaned over, picked up a beer, tossed it in the air, and caught it on the third spin, then pulled a knife from God knew where and stabbed the can. "Make a seal with your lips and suck like you've never sucked before." He looked so naughty right now as he made the hole bigger with his knife and pushed in the sharp edges of the blue Bud Light can.

"I have to suck it all at once?"

"Fuck yes. It's practice for when you suck my d—"

"Okay, I get it!"

Jathan handed it to her carefully on its side so it wouldn't spill, stabbed his own, then showed her how to tilt her head back and pop the top to relieve the pressure. Lynn was belly laughing so hard, she couldn't do it. She had to take a few breaths before she brought the can to her lips.

"Ready," Jathan said, smile bright white in the night shadows. "Steady... Go!"

Lynn popped the top and chugged, but it took her way longer than Jathan. For a second, she felt bad until he started cheering her on. She had to stop once because of laughter and spilled a little on the ground, but she finished it. Sure, it was silly, but she was kind of proud of herself. Especially with Jathan lifting her up and spinning her in a circle like she'd just won a damn Olympic game.

He kissed her and then licked her chin with the tippy tip of his tongue. "You have beer on your face."

"You've seen me worse," Lynn deadpanned.

"I didn't say I didn't like it. Fiery, redheaded, badass panther shifter who tastes like beer? Hell yes to all that. Next clue. Get on my quad." He jerked his chin toward the four-wheeler.

"You make everything sound filthy."

"Hidden talents, Lynn. I'm gonna make you fall in love with me."

Ha. Too late.

Lynn rushed upstairs, pulled on a lacey thong, a pair of jeans, and a tight T-shirt she hadn't felt good enough to wear in a long time. She did a quick tie of her hiking boots, and then she jogged down the stairs back to her Knight in Shining Holey Jeans.

Jathan squeezed her ass hard as she got on the ATV. She giggled the entire way up the trail to Bear Trap Falls, and when they ended up at the beach by the river, right by where the water dropped off the cliff, she thought maybe this was the best night of her whole life. The moon was full and bright, the stars speckling the sky, not a cloud in sight, and even though the breeze was chilly, she was flushed with the adventure and didn't feel the cold. There were two more beers on a flat rock with a letter squeezed in between them. Lynn scrambled for it.

"Last clue," she read aloud as Jathan shut off the four-wheeler behind her. "Time to take a leap of faith, little scrapper. Down this beer and jump. Your dinner is under the falls. Also, Jathan wet the bed until he was ten, is terrible at sharing food, and had reoccurring dreams about chickens chasing him until he graduated high school. Ask him what his biggest fear is."

"Chickens," Jathan muttered without hesitation as he wrapped his arms around her waist and rested his chin on her shoulder. "They freak me out."

Lynn belted out a laugh and finished reading. "Are you sure you still want to deal with all of that? Just making sure. Your tacos are probably soggy. Maybe it will make Jathan not suck at sharing. Sorry for earlier. I wanted you to remember how to fight. I wanted you to live. Willa."

Lynn swallowed a few times to try to control her emotions. They were swinging so far and wide right now. Jathan stabbed the beers, made the holes bigger, and they shotgunned their second blue cans. She did better this time and was feeling buzzed.

"Ready?" Jathan asked, stripping out of his shirt and kicking out of his boots. He left his jeans on, so she did the same. No shirt, but the pants and lacy bra stayed.

"Ready," she said.

"Thata girl," Jathan said quietly before he pulled her to his chest. For a few moments, he searched her eyes before he leaned down and kissed her. Giant, dominant, tatted-up bad boy who turned gentle with a touch for her. He was the most surprising man she'd ever met. As he sipped at her lips, such a strange sensation took her. It was butterflies in her stomach and an unfamiliar ache in her chest. And the more he kissed her, the sharper the pain in her heart became until she gasped and flinched back.

"Hurts," Jathan said, head still angled like he would kiss her again. His eyes were on her swollen lips, and he was smiling.

"Yeah."

Jathan frowned slightly. "All this time, I thought it didn't exist."

"What didn't?" she whispered, gripping onto his strong arms to stay steady.

He pressed his lips against her forehead, let them linger there for the span of three breaths, and then he released her and ran for the edge of the falls. As he jumped over the side of the cliff, he spun in the air to face her and called out, "The bond, Lynn." And then his smiling face disappeared.

She ran to the edge just in time to see him sink into the waves below. He'd probably jumped off this cliff a thousand times. The bond? Lynn pressed the flat of her palm against her chest and shook her head. Couldn't be...could it? She'd never felt this with Brody. She ran her fingertips over the healing claiming mark, tracing Jathan's bite. And it hit her. Tonight had been so up and down, so emotionally draining, and then they'd gone right into the scavenger hunt. This was her first moment alone when she could come to grips with everything that happened.

He'd claimed her. She was his and he was hers. And where was Monster? Where was the blinking and losing time? Oh, she wasn't cured. She was still messed up and probably always would be, but she was standing here, present, smiling like a lunatic, tracing a claiming mark from someone she loved. Really loved.

Her life had flipped so fast it had stolen her breath away. And right now, she wanted to revel in this moment of freedom and not worry about anything. Not tomorrow, or the pressure, or the work that lay ahead. She wanted to eat dinner with her mate—*her mate*—under a waterfall and pretend they were both normal and undamaged for just one night. Because with Jathan, he made her feel...okay.

She inhaled deeply, blew her breath out twice, and then let out a whoop as she ran for the edge. She threw her arms out and flew for a few breathtaking seconds, before she put her hands together and dove into the water. She wanted to cry and laugh and yell with elation because she'd never in a million years thought she could feel this again—joy.

She swam for the surface and broke the waves with a gasp. And Jathan was there, grinning so big she wanted to kiss him just to taste that smile. He inhaled deeply, then sank below the waves, and she followed. Streaks of blue moonlight striped the water, and it sparkled when the light hit tiny pieces of sediment. Jathan led them to the waterfall where billions of bubbles were racing toward the surface from where the river above pounded into the river below. He swam deeper under the falls and disappeared, and for a second, she panicked. Her breath was almost gone, and she didn't know whether to go back up or keep following him.

She trusted Jathan though, so she pushed on, and right on the other side, she kicked upward and found the surface. Breath heaving, she made her way to the edge of a rock shelf where she'd spent hours talking with the kids from Damon's Mountains when her foster parents brought her here for visits. This place was full of happy memories. They echoed in her mind—children's laughter, her laughter.

Jathan stood in his soaking jeans, abs flexing with every breath, longer dark hair on top messy and dripping, skin glowing blue where the moonlight crept in the sides of the waterfall. He was stunning, but it wasn't the muscles or tattoos or the height. It was the way he looked at her, like she was important. Like she really was redeemable.

"Are we really bonded?" she asked, gripping the edge of the rocks and kicking against the current.

Jathan bent down and pulled her out of the water, settled her on her feet, and brushed wet tendrils of hair out of her face. "Your hair is always wild. I like it because it's so...you."

Did he not hear her question?

Jathan's gaze dipped to her lips, and his eyes

went serious. "Brody told you that you two were bonded, right?"

She dipped her chin once.

"So me telling you we're bonded isn't the answer you need. That is something you need to feel for yourself."

"I do feel different. There's something in my chest. In my heart. I feel steadier, like you are pulling the darkness from me and calming Monster."

Jathan ran his hands up and down her arms quickly, as if trying to warm her, but she hadn't even noticed her gooseflesh until he did that. "Date number two and three. An almost dinner with my crazy parents, and soggy tacos and whiskey. You're a lucky woman, Lynn."

"I know you're being sarcastic, but I really am lucky. And also hungry."

There were three battery-powered lanterns on a blanket, and in the middle was Clinton's flask, two paper plates, and a bag of food. Best date ever.

Jathan was talking about how he was glad they included extra hot sauce, but a breeze lifted the soaking ends of her hair and the scent of something familiar hit her nose. When she turned, the back of the waterfall wavered and changed. It morphed to the clearing of the cabins in Red Havoc Territory. She could hear crying on the wind, just the softest sob, and then Lynn saw her. Eden. Her bird. Her best friend. The albino falcon shifter who had been so determined to save her. She was sitting on the front steps of Lynn's old cabin, staring off into the woods, crying.

Lynn didn't know how she knew, but Eden was crying for her.

Two cabins down, Barret, the panther she'd dragged into that lion war, was standing with his shoulder propped on the side of his cabin, watching Eden cry. He looked like he hadn't slept in weeks, and his eyes were full of ghosts. Such a bone-deep feeling of homesickness hit Lynn right in the gut.

Her people were hurting while she was here.

Firm hands gripped her shoulders, and the mirage wavered to the back of the waterfall again.

"Lynn. Lynn, talk to me. Stay with me."

With a frown, she gave her attention to Jathan.

"Are you still here with me?" he asked, worry pooling in his dark eyes.

"Yes, I'm still here."

He huffed a sigh of relief and pulled her against his chest, hugged her up tight. His heartbeat banged against her cheek as she stared at the waterfall and remembered the tone of Eden's heartache.

Lynn was still here with him for now.

But soon...very soon...if she really wanted to get better, she would have to go home and face the crew she'd left behind.

ELEVEN

Lynn hid like a coward behind a pine with a wide, knobby trunk. She hadn't been back to her parent's house in so long, and it felt strange, like déjà vu. She had planned on being the badass Jathan thought she was and march right up to the front door and knock, just like she belonged. But when she'd walked down here from her tree house, three miles of woods, the first thing she saw when she came to the house she'd grown up in was Jathan's motorcycle.

She'd thought he was working. It was lunch time, so maybe he was on a break from hauling logs.

He'd taught her how to be brave, but she wanted to do this part alone, and then afterward, she wanted to fall apart alone. It was a hard balance, this recovery. She waffled between needing Jathan to prop her up and keeping him from becoming her backbone. She needed to do some of the work alone so that she could be proud when she came out of this. And she *would* come out of this.

The door to her parent's house opened, and Jathan ducked under the low doorframe. He was wearing a black tank top with mud stains across the front and worn jeans over his work boots, both spattered with the dirty remnants of last night's rainstorm. He wore a distracted smile and was saying something too low for her to hear from where she stood in the cool shadows of the tree. He was a huge and intimidating man. Sometimes she forgot how big he was until she saw him standing next to someone else. And when her mom came out of the house after him, a foot and a half shorter than him, she was overwhelmed with the urge to laugh and sigh with relief all at once. Mom. God, it was good to see her.

She'd pulled her dark hair up in a messy bun, and her eyes crinkled at the corners as she looked up at Jathan and responded to something he'd said. Her dad came out next, but Lynn couldn't even look at his face. Her attention was devoted to the little, precious baby he carried in his arms.

Lynn crouched immediately because she was overwhelmed and wouldn't stay standing for long anyway. One year old. Amberlynn was so beautiful, crop of red hair the same shade as Lynn's on her head, eyes the same shade of soft brown as hers, too. She looked absolutely nothing like Brody.

Lynn blew out a silent, shaking breath as her eyes filled with tears. *My babyyyy*. A purr rattled up her throat. A purr? God, how long had it been since she made that happy sound? It tickled.

Amberlynn was smiling a big gummy grin at Jathan who was covering his face, then uncovering it. Peekaboo. He reached for Lynn's baby girl as though he'd done it a million times and pulled her against his chest. And then he did something that stunned her. Jathan, big bad bear who never attached to anyone, hugged her daughter close, hand on the back of her head as he rocked back and forth and talked to Lynn's parents. Amberlynn was soooo tiny in his big, tattooed arms, and she settled against him instantly.

Oh, Jathan had given that little girl his heart. Lynn could see it clear as day.

Her arms itched to be the one holding her.

Jathan gave the baby back to her mom, and as he jogged down the stairs with a wave, Lynn did a Monster check. In her middle, the cat was quiet and watchful. Not the foul demon she was most of the time.

The rumble of Jathan's bike engine was loud in the quiet clearing. One more two-fingered wave, and then he was blasting off down the road. Her parents watched him go. They used to do that with her when she would leave. They always waited until she was completely gone before they went back inside. It made her smile. They liked Jathan, and something about that made her really happy. Had he told them they'd bonded? Had he told them he'd claimed her, or that she'd claimed him back?

Had he told them he was trying to save their daughter?

This felt like date number four, and he didn't even realize she'd been here.

Be brave.

Lynn stood and walked out of the shadows, eyes on her mom's face. Mom jerked her attention to Lynn, and her lips parted in shock. "Lynn?" she asked in a hopeful voice. "Lynn?" she asked louder, bolting down the steps, holding tight to Amberlynn.

Lynn lost it, just bawling, as she ran to her mom and threw her arms around her and her little girl. "I'm sorry," she whispered brokenly. "I'm sorry I pushed you away. I'm sorry I didn't come back. I'm sorry—"

"Shhhh," her mom crooned.

"I'm sorry for everything."

Another pair of arms went around them. Dad. Tears streaming down her face, Lynn rested her cheek on her dad's chest. He'd always been the strongest man she knew, but even he was tearing up. He kissed the top of her head three times quick and hugged her tighter.

"Ba!" Amberlynn said.

The noise startled Lynn. Not because it was loud, but because even if she hadn't seen her baby in a hundred years, she would recognize her voice, down to her bones, down to her base instincts. That little voice was for her. It was Lynn's call.

Lynn eased back and smiled through her tears at Amberlynn. *My baby, my baby, my babyyyy.*

"Can I hold her?" Lynn whispered, hopeful

but terrified of rejection.

"Are you okay right now?"

Lynn winced at the pain Mom's question caused, but she understood. They were the ones keeping Amberlynn safe right now—even if that meant from Lynn.

"Oh, honey," Mom said, cupping her chin. "You pushed us away, but we didn't stay away. We've been following everything. Ben kept us updated, and when you came back to Damon's Mountains, Jathan started visiting. He's good. He cares about you, we can tell. He tells us you're gonna get better, but you're still hurting." Mom looked down at Amberlynn, then held her out to Lynn.

For a second, Lynn was shocked. The moment was here. She was going to get to touch her baby. What if she was bad at this? What if she didn't remember how to be a mom? Monster check: still quiet.

Lynn reached for her and pulled her to her hip. She rocked with a little bounce as

Amberlynn frowned up at her. Of course she wouldn't recognize her. It hurt, but that was on Lynn, not Amberlynn. When she pressed her thumb against Amberlynn's little hand, the girl wrapped her chubby little fingers around her and squeezed. Lynn gave off a relieved sigh at how good it felt. It was like the best hug she'd ever had, plus a drink of water after a week in the desert, plus her soul being filled with joy—all at the same time. It was beautiful.

"What will you do?" Mom asked softly, her eyes on where Amberlynn and Lynn were holding hands.

"What do you think I should do?"

"Live. Of course live, baby. I was so—" Mom's voice hitched, and she swallowed hard before she continued. "You *scared* us. What should you do? Work toward a good life. That's all we've ever wanted for you. To be happy." She twitched her head toward the road where Jathan had disappeared. "Starting with that one was a smart move. We are just Amberlynn's grandparents.

She needs her mom."

Lynn bit her lip hard to keep her face from crumpling. She hadn't been called a mom in a while. "I'm not ready yet. I wish I could take her now. Right now. I wish I could walk her right back to where I live and be good enough for her. But I'm at the beginning..."

"We know you are," Dad rumbled. Big cat shifter with the same snarly voice she'd grown up listening to. "You did good, girl. You brought her to us when you knew you couldn't keep her safe. We're family. We did our job while you were hurting, but now you have a bigger job. Recover, Lynn. Don't be one of the shifters who has to be put down. It'll break so many hearts. Be that tough-as-leather panther we raised. The one we can't live without. The one we adopted because you made our family whole. It's time to make your family whole now."

"Three months," Lynn promised, feeling liquid steel fill her veins. "Give me three months, and I'll be ready for her, I'll be whole, and I'll be enough. I'm gonna put in the work. I'm gonna do this for her." Even she could hear the conviction ringing clear as a bell in her voice.

Dad lifted his chin and smiled, his blue eyes dancing with pride. "There's the Lynn I know."

TWELVE

"Oh, my gosh," Lynn muttered as she nearly busted her ass on the stairs to the treehouse.

The plethora of grocery bags on her arms were to blame. This staircase was way too narrow for her to make this in one trip, but she was a get-shit-doner now, so she muscled the bags up the stairs like a boss-B and went to kick the door open like a ninja-badass, but the sound of a chainsaw made her stop mid-kick.

"What the hell?" Panicked, she pushed her way through the door and locked her legs in the entryway. She stared dumbfoundedly at one very sexy, but very confusing, man in front of her. Jathan was all white T-shirt, bulging muscles, and...safety goggles? He was also currently cutting a chunk out of her wall—the part with the countdown marks.

"What are you doing?" she yelled over the noise.

"Erasing this fucking reminder. Did you get ice cream sandwiches?"

"What? Why would I get ice cream sandwiches?"

"Because they're delicious."

Sawdust was flying everywhere, all over the floor, all over her bed that she'd actually made today. She'd just swept the whole treehouse. "Jathan, you ridiculous Neanderthal! I just cleaned this place!"

The perfect square of the tally marks fell onto the floor with a *clump*. "It looks great in here," he said, turning off the chainsaw.

She offered him a slow blink.

"I brought matches and gasoline. You wanna

set a fire?" he asked, shoving the safety glasses up on his head.

"Why?"

"Why do you keep asking why? Fires are awesome."

"Well…" She looked around at the mess. "I was going to cook dinner but I guess we can…set…fires?"

"Wait," he said, tucking his chin to his chest and giving her a sexy come-hither look. "You can cook?"

Lynn snorted. "I used to. I have to remember how to do it. Greyson and Barret were feeding me frozen bean burritos and peanut butter sandwiches for the last year. I want spaghetti. I texted you." She got suddenly shy and made her way to the kitchen to unload her arms. Clearing her throat, she tried again. "I texted to see if you wanted to eat here. You know…for our next date."

Jathan's dark eyebrows shot up nearly to his hairline, and his eyes danced with amusement.

"Are you asking me out?"

"Yes." Her cheeks were on fire so she ducked her gaze to hide the blush.

"That's very forward of you, Lynn. I mean, we've only had sex one time. Asking me out is a big deal."

"You're being a turd."

"False, turds can't set fires." Jathan left the chainsaw in a pile of sawdust and approached her quick. He lifted her up in the air so she was looking down at him. The light from the kitchen window made his brown eyes look lighter.

"What are we burning?" she asked softly, brushing her fingertips down his beard.

"That countdown. Your past. Burn it all— we're starting over. How many times did you Change today?"

Lynn sighed because she didn't want him to be disappointed in her. "Twice."

"On purpose?"

"Grr, I don't want to talk about this. I want to make spaghetti and fuck against the wall."

Jathan chuckled. "All right, you little boner fairy, stop. Tell me the bad stuff first so we can get to the fun stuff."

Lynn snarled up her lip, but she could see he wasn't going to let her off the hook. "I Changed, but not on purpose. Monster is still Monster."

"Disagree. Two times is better than the fifteen a day you were doing last week. Did you find someone to fight?"

She shook her head. "I just shredded some trees and pissed in Clinton's yard. Twice."

"Good. You're doing better and so is Monster. How many times did you check out?"

"Jathan," she whispered, pleading.

The smile fell from his face. "How many?" he asked in a harder tone.

"Four. It was an emotional day."

"How so?"

"I saw you on your lunch break."

"You saw me—?"

She could practically see the lightbulb go off over his head.

"Oooh," he drawled out. "You saw her? You saw Amberlynn today?"

Her chest was too tight, so she inhaled deeply to try to loosen it. "All the disappearing and Changes happened after I left my parents' house."

Jathan slid her down him until she was steady on her feet. "And?"

"I saw you hold her." She was too chicken to look in his eyes right now, so she smiled at his chest instead. "And then I held her."

"I'm so damn proud of you right now." Jathan's voice shook slightly. "You did that on your own. And look at this." He lifted her hand. "Bright pink nails?"

"I felt adventurous. I got a manicure and pedicure and I drank one glass of wine. And then I got this coffee with chocolate in it because I was so tired after the big day, which made me feel all crazy, so then I went grocery shopping and bought everything because I was hungry but I didn't get any ice cream sandwiches. I bought candy bars to put in the freezer instead. I like to eat them frozen."

"I've never tried that. Okay, date-night here. Setting fire to your countdown. Pasta. Definitely fucking against a wall...and maybe over there in that chair, also on the kitchen table, in that pile of sawdust... And frozen candy bars."

Before she could chicken out and change her mind, she blurted, "And tomorrow I'll go home."

Jathan flinched back like she'd pushed him. "What do you mean you'll go home?"

"Back to Red Havoc. Back to my crew. I owe Barret an apology. A big one. And I need to go back and be with my people."

"Your people."

She nodded. "I have no crew here. I think I need Red Havoc to finish getting better."

Jathan took a few steps back and huffed a humorless laugh as he scratched his earlobe in an irritated gesture. "You have no crew here? You have me, Lynn." He pulled up the sleeve of his shirt to expose the healed bite mark on his bicep. "What am I supposed to do?"

"No, you don't understand." She had a letter. She'd written it for him. In the parking lot of the grocery store, she'd sat in the car she'd borrowed from her parents and poured her heart out into a letter that would explain everything way better than she could do with words.

"Fuck, Lynn. You're leaving? There's war waiting for you in Red Havoc, and you'll go without me. Just leave me here to what? Go back to logging? Go back to being alone? Go back to my fucking nothing life that I thought was so great and so perfect before you came along and ruined that? We're bonded! You can't just go anymore!" His fists were clenched, and red was creeping up his neck.

"I'll fix it, I'll fix it, just..." Her vision was getting dark at the edges, and a snarl bubbled out of her throat. Fuck. "No, no, no, everything will be okay." Where the fuck was the letter? She rifled through the bags desperately.

"I don't want you to go without me. I put everything into making you live, and now you'll just go? And live without me? I was fucked up too! I am fucked up. No one gets me but you. You're really leaving? You're really leaving." His voice dipped low and panicked. "Oh my God, you're really leaving." Jathan ran his hands through his hair and strode toward the door.

"Jath—!" She choked on his name as her hand rested on the letter, sitting on top of a package of diapers she was going to drop by her parents in the morning when she said goodbye. Her hands clenched as the door slammed closed...

Blink. Time was lost.

****

God, he was so pissed. No, not pissed. This was something more. This was something Jathan didn't understand.

It was fear.

"Fuck!" he yelled at the top of his lungs.

He couldn't leave her like this, not in an argument. He needed to calm down and understand why she didn't want him.

Gripping the railing of the staircase, he heaved breath and glared at the dandelions in the front yard, trying to get his bear under control. He'd left so he wouldn't have an uncontrolled Change in her treehouse, but he couldn't give himself to the bear right now. He had to fix whatever got broken between them because, goddammit, he loved her. He *loved* her. All of her flaws were so fucking beautiful to him. She was perfect. Perfectly broken to fit him. He didn't have to pretend to be normal with her. Her damage matched his. She didn't even blink at his faults. He couldn't just rampage out of here and go grizzly, looking for a fight. His fight needed to be for her right now.

With a snarl, he squeezed his eyes closed against the blinding sunlight and the pounding headache forming behind his eyes. *Come on, Monster. Let me keep this skin a while longer so I can get her back.*

He clenched his fists to stop the trembling,

then turned and made his way back up the stairs. But when he went back inside, Lynn wasn't there. "Lynn?" He scanned the small space, but he didn't hear anything or see her anywhere.

Baffled, he made his way into the kitchen, and there she was on the floor. "Shit. Lynn?" He pulled her head into his lap, but she was just staring vacantly at the cabinets. In her hand was a folded piece of paper. Her fingers covered most of the writing on the outside, but he could see the last four letters. *Than.* His name was on there.

Cradling her body in his lap, he plucked the letter from her fingertips and opened it up.

Dear Jathan,

I saw you hold my baby today. It was one of my most favorite moments of my whole life. I went to my parents because it was something I needed to do alone. You've gotten me as far as you can. Let me explain. I don't want all my strength to come from our bond or from you. I need some of that strength to come from inside of me, so I never fall again. I'm ready to make changes and excited about the future...with you. Give me a week with Red Havoc to make my apologies and put in some work. Work on me. Because you deserve a mate who is whole and strong. I look up to you. You are steady, even though I can see your fight with your animal. You are so motivating. You got me here, Jathan. You got me fighting. Now I need a minute to finish this fight. One week, and then I'm going to call you, and I'm going to beg you to come to Red Havoc territory. I'm going to be selfish and ask you to leave your job here, your crew, your life here, and pledge to a panther shifter alpha. Greyson is good to his bones, like you are. I'm going to justify it by telling myself your brother is in my crew, and you'll he happier there with me and him. I've told my parents three months, and I'll be ready to bring Amberlynn home to Red Havoc. You are my mate, Jathan. Maybe you always were. Maybe something deep inside of me told me that when we kissed at that party all those years ago. And maybe all that bad stuff happened because we needed to end up here, in this moment, fighting for each other, fighting with each other, back to back, just me and you against the world. Today, I Changed right after I left Amberlynn, and Monster wanted to fight you. You. I couldn't get that out of my head. It scared me.

"Jesus," Jathan murmured, stroking Lynn's hair. That was one side of Beaston's vision. That she would fight him, and Jathan would be the one to end her. They had to stay far, far away from that scenario. If her growth was capped here, then she was making the right decision. God, it hurt to think about her leaving him, but at least she was giving him a time limit. She was going to ask him to come along. She wasn't leaving, not really. She was being strong.

Scrubbing his hand down his beard, he continued.

For a second, I wanted to run from you. Not

because I was scared you would hurt me, but because I was afraid of hurting you. But I'm not running. That's not what this is. I'm going to make you a big dinner and have a perfect night with you. And then I'm going to pack my things and go back to the Appalachian Mountains and do work on myself that will make you proud.

I know we haven't said the L word yet, and I'm kind of scared to tell anyone this again, but you're different. You earned my trust. So I'll be brave, because you deserve a brave mate. I told you that love is fire. That love will burn you to the ground, and for a while, I truly believed that. But you've taught me that while all love is fire, only some of it will burn you to the ground. You'll keep me from burning, and I'll do the same for you.

I love you.

-Lynn

THIRTEEN

Lynn eased her eyes open, but the room was as dark as it had been behind her eyelids. Where was she? The scent of sawdust, her sheets, and Jathan eased her confusion. His hand was resting on her waist, big and strong and warm. And then she remembered the fight. She'd disappeared.

"Are you back?" he asked in a sleep-filled, rumbling voice.

"How long was I gone?"

The mattress sank behind her and the sheets ripped off her legs as he rolled over to check the alarm clock. "Six hours. That was a long one."

"At least I didn't Change and try to murder people. Bright side."

Jathan chuckled, slid his hand back over her waist, and pulled her against his chest. He plucked at the back of her neck with little, biting kisses. "I packed your things," he murmured against her skin. "I didn't understand, but I read your letter. And I think you're right. You went from being dependent on your parents, to dependent on Brody, to dependent on Greyson and Barret, to depending on me. As much as I don't want you to go, I understand why you have to."

"I'm sorry—"

"Shhh. I'm not mad. I'm proud of you." He rolled his hips against her, and his erection pressed against her spine, causing her to arch back on instinct. "You're so fucking sexy when I see that fight in you, Lynn. When I see you pushing to be better." Another roll of his hips. "Badass looks good on you."

A purr rattled up her throat as she reached

behind her and clutched onto his bare thigh. "Wait." She frowned. "Am I naked?"

"You're welcome. It's hot as fuck in here. I don't know how you sleep with any clothes on."

She giggled and wiggled back closer to him. "So, you didn't undress me while I was checked out because you're a perv?"

"Well yeah, I'm a perv too, but mostly it was for un-selfish reasons. You need central air, or at least a damn window unit. Sleeping with the window open isn't cutting it, and there's this single damn mosquito that's been buzzing around my head all night. It took all my inner strength not to take you to my trailer so it doesn't feel like I'm sleeping in a bonfire, but me dragging your limp body around the trailer park would look suspicious. Plus, I've seen you naked like four thousand times this month. You Changed so much, you are basically a nudist. Also, I didn't figure you would mind me undressing you on account of me putting my pecker in you yesterday."

She gave a belly laugh as he pressed his lips to her neck again. His hands were gentle, then rough, gentle, then rough. Soft touches on her hips, her breasts, her belly, and then a hard grip on one hip, and he slammed his body against hers. His touch trailed fire across her skin. Up her ribs to her breasts where he cupped and squeezed as he pulled her against him even harder.

What was he waiting for? She was ready right now, but time and time again, he got rough on her skin, then eased back and touched her soft again. She bowed her back, pleading silently, but he didn't push into her. "Jathan, please."

"Impatient," he accused, and then clamped his teeth on the back of her neck like he was punishing her. This was a punishment she could get on board with, though. She froze and moaned as he bit down harder. Rough, dominant man. Did he even realize how much control he had over Monster? She was writhing inside of Lynn. In her mind's eye, Monster was rubbing against her mate's leg. He was making her completely devoted with a touch. Good Bear.

Rough, soft...rough, soft.

She lifted one leg and eased her ankle back over his knee, spreading her legs for him. He eased back just a little, and when he rocked his hips against her this time, the head of his cock was right there, swollen, pushing into her easy because she was so ready.

Jathan pulled out, but she chased him. "Deeper," she whispered.

A soft growl rattled through his chest and vibrated against her back. He slid his hand around her hip, down her leg, to her inner thigh and yanked her legs open wider with a firm grasp, his fingers digging in. And then he reared back and slammed into her so deep she gasped. Reaching back behind her, she gripped his neck as he pounded into her again. Teeth on her skin. Teeth, teeth. She rolled her eyes closed and moved with him. His hand slid from her inner thigh to her sex where he cupped her as he thrust into her again. The pleasure built so fast. She was getting close. He'd worked her up so high, she was toeing the edge of release, unable to find a single word to warn him that she was already there.

As if he knew, he rolled her over until her chest was on the bed, her arms curled under her, her ass in the air. And then he bucked into her deep, hard, again and again, fast where before he'd been going too slow. His fist hit the bed next to her shoulder, and he snarled as he worked them both to that that moment of utter exhilaration. Utter release. She let go, offered her control to him, closed her eyes to the world, and let him shatter her body. Owned. He owned her body, and how beautiful that, after everything, she had the capability to trust someone like this again.

Faster and faster, he bucked into her until she was there, screaming his name. Her body clenched around him, and he drove deep pulsing heat into her as he gritted out a guttural, sexy sound. "Mine," he snarled.

"Yours," she said breathlessly. Always.

Jathan slowed, but Lynn kept her focus on the throbbing warmth between them. On where they were connected. On where he was drawing every single aftershock from her until she was spent and exhausted and full of him. The strange sensation in her chest was back, but it wasn't painful.

Jathan eased out of her and turned her over gently, as if coveting her. He intertwined his fingers with hers and pressed her hands into the mattress above her head. As he eased into the space between her legs, he searched her face with the softest expression. Even in the dark, she could see his eyes were still brown. Maybe she settled his animal like he settled hers. Slowly, he leaned down and hesitated, his lips only an inch from hers. God, she loved him. Loved this. She tilted her chin up and pressed her mouth to his. He slid his tongue past her lips and took his time with each stroke into her mouth. Lynn could almost taste his devotion. Big, tatted-up, mountain of a grizzly shifter, and he went gentle and considerate with her. Only her.

She felt like a goddess.

She felt powerful and beautiful.

She felt like a badass because he reminded her that she was and encouraged her to fight. Strength didn't intimidate a man like Jathan. Not like it had with Brody.

She was able to be herself with this man, and there was something so freeing about that. Her conviction that love would burn her to the ground wasn't true with him.

He'd changed everything.

Fixed her most broken pieces.

Fixed her as much as he could.

And tomorrow, he would let her go to fix herself the rest of the way, and he wasn't threatened by growth that wouldn't include him.

Good Bear.

FOURTEEN

Lynn didn't like goodbyes, so she didn't do them. Instead, she left little thank you letters on everyone's doorsteps like some apology Easter Bunny. She'd said sorry to everyone she'd fought and thanked them for being patient with Monster. She had thanked Creed for taking her in, Willa for pushing her to pick a side of the fence, and Beaston for being on the edge of most of the fights, ready to protect her like Jathan had been.

She'd had so many shifters in Damon's Mountains pulling for her, and she hadn't even realized it until she could think straight again. Nobody had ended her, despite her begging, because on some level, they believed in her. And now she believed in herself, too. Why? Because she'd seen so much improvement in just a week. Was this work easy? Hell no, and she still had her weak moments, but she'd gained traction and was motivated. She imagined herself this snowball on a hill. She'd taken a long time to roll off the edge, but now she was mid-way down, going faster, growing, with more force than she knew she possessed. She just needed to keep it up, keep striving for that improvement.

Jathan had gone to work at the landing early this morning. They'd had sex again as soon as he woke up, and this time he was gentle. That man surprised her in the best ways. Jathan's goodbye letter she left on the door to his trailer was much simpler than the others because it wasn't a goodbye. It was a see-you-soon. All it said was:

We're still here with you.

- Lynn & Monster

And she was. Jathan was filling up a lot of real estate in her heart, and her thoughts orbited around him. Around their future. She was going to set them up in Red Havoc. Her body would be in the Appalachians with her crew, but her heart would remain here with her man.

Mason, Damon Daye's boar shifter best friend and assistant, waited for her patiently under the Grayland Mobile Park sign, holding open the door to a black Lincoln Town Car. He wasn't dressed in his usual work garb, though. Today was holey jeans and a navy blue T-shirt with some beer logo she'd never heard of. He hadn't shaved, and a touch of silver showed in his beard.

"Morning," he rumbled with a smile. "You ready to go home?"

With one last look at the Grayland Mobile Park, Lynn huffed a steadying sigh and nodded.

She shoved her heavy duffle bag into the back seat, and then lifted the package of diapers to show him. "I have one stop to make on the way to the airport. Do we have time?"

Mason grinned. "That we do. Are those for Clinton?"

Lynn laughed and shook her head as she crawled into the back seat. She cradled Medusa in her lap and stared out the window as Mason drove them out of Damon's Mountains. But right before they hit the main road, he slammed on the brakes. Lynn gasped as they skidded to a stop only inches away from hitting Beaston. He stood there stock still, tall, lean, dark hair, bright green eyes the same shade of Jathan's when he was riled up. Beaston had his head cocked to the side and was staring through the dark tinted front window, as if he could see right into Lynn's soul. Gooseflesh rose on her arms as he stalked slowly to her door.

Swallowing hard, she rolled down the window.

"I found this," Beaston said in a gravelly voice. He lifted the letter she'd left shoved in between the door and frame of his singlewide. Then he locked his arms against the open window. "You thanked me."

"I meant it."

"You said I was good."

Lynn nodded. "You protected me when I was weak."

Beaston huffed a sound she couldn't interpret. "Weak. Weak? Lynn of Red Havoc, Lynn, the queen of the broken and the fixed, Lynn the ghost...do you know what your panther is?"

"A monster?" she whispered.

Beaston straightened his spine. "I see ghosts. I always saw you. You can go away when things get hard, but you never disappear completely. And while you did that, you broke your panther into a weapon. You are exactly as you are supposed to be. You did good getting here. You said I was good. You're good, too."

Lynn frowned. "What do you mean?"

"You can get her back."

"Amberlynn?" God, she couldn't keep up with what he was saying. She was so confused.

"Not until the crew of two wars is the crew of two wars won. Stay near Greyson in that fight. Two ghost cats. Stay near your alpha and protect his neck. Save Red Havoc. You were born to be exactly this. No one else could fall apart, rebuild, fall apart, and rebuild like you did. You were born to be tested. You were born to save the people you love." A slow, feral smile curved Beaston's lips. "No more giving anyone your neck, *Monster*. Now you be the ripper."

With that, he turned and walked into the woods without a single look back. And at the tree line, he disappeared as if he'd never been there at all. She scanned the woods with her hunter eyes, but he never showed up again between the trees.

"Did you understand any of that?" she asked Mason.

"Beaston is man of few words, Lynn. He told you exactly what you need to know, and nothing more. You got a fight comin', girl. Better get your head on right."

What the shit? She'd thought the fight was hers, within her, and now she was supposed to save people outside of herself?

She'd had a plan. Get better and keep the ones she loved. Keep Jathan, keep Amberlynn, keep Red Havoc. And now Beaston had taken that plan and crushed it under his boot like a bug.

Rage was a slow boil in her blood as Mason hit the gas and the woods blurred by. Lynn left the window open to feel the breeze on her flushed cheeks as she chewed on her thumbnail and lost herself to the swirling questions Beaston had conjured.

She was supposed to be like this? How utterly unfair. Everyone else got to be normal with normal shifter problems. Not blinking and losing time, or losing control of their animals, or getting so warped in the mind and eaten with guilt that they almost got an early end. She was almost one of those crazy shifters who got put down for the good of others. So close.

Crazy Lynn—she was really supposed to be Crazy Lynn? More questions... Beaston had visions that came true, so she really would get Amberlynn back? After some war she had no clue about? Be the ripper? Protect her alpha? She could barely take care of herself!

But one question repeated in her head over and over until she was consumed with it.

Who the hell was hunting her crew?

FIFTEEN

Well, that was the fanciest fucking experience she'd ever had in her entire life.

Lynn stood on the side of the airport runway and stared at the small private jet Damon had chartered for her to get back to Red Havoc territory. They'd landed a while ago, and then she'd just stood here for probably the last five minutes trying to wrap her head around the experience she'd just had. They'd fed her caviar, like in the movies. And she had sipped champagne like a fancy lady and even remembered to hold her wine flute with one pinky up so she could take a selfie for Eden, her best friend. She'd texted it to her, and the only response she'd gotten was, *OMG, wherethefuckareyou and is that a smile I see?!?!!!!!!! Lynn?!! YOU LOOK BEAUTIFUL AND I CAN'T WAIT TO SEE YOU AND SERIOUSLY WHERETHEFUCKAREYOU????*

Eeeeh, she hadn't been the best at keeping her crew updated on her progress apparently. Now she felt really bad for worrying them. She definitely needed to work on her friendship skills.

Damon had probably put her on a private jet so she didn't Change in a human flight and bite people. She hoped Monster wasn't capable of that, but she might be. Caviar. That was crazy. And awesome. And before they served her a lavish dinner, they'd even given her a hot towel. She hadn't known what to do with it, but the stewardess told her to wash her hands with it. She put it on her face when the lady wasn't looking though, because it felt good. She probably shouldn't have worn booty shorts and a faded red T-shirt that said *aliens exist* with little cartoon extraterrestrials on it, but then again, she hadn't known Damon had hooked her up with this fancy flight either.

The airport must be a private one, because it was tiny, with just one runway, and only a few small planes that looked like the one she'd just landed in.

After she rounded the corner, adjusting the strap of her duffle bag, she spotted Ben beside his truck at the edge of the parking lot. There was no smile on his face. There was worry, trepidation perhaps. He looked wary and weary, his eyes the bright gold of his panther. She hesitated, faltered a few steps, then made her way to him.

"Tell me you're upright again, Lynn," he said in a low voice. His eyes were hollow. They looked like Barret's in that vision, as though he hadn't slept since she'd left Red Havoc Territory.

No tears. Time to find your backbone.

Lynn straightened up and lifted her chin. She wished she could say yes, but he would hear her lie. So instead, she said, "I'm getting there."

Benson Saber, the previous alpha of the Red Havoc Crew, now the Second of the Red Havoc Crew, the man who took her in, took her under his wing, deflated with a huff of emotional breath. "Thank God," he murmured and pulled her against him roughly. She couldn't breathe but she didn't care right now. She hadn't allowed touch in the year before Jathan, and it had hurt her. She hadn't realized that until now. Ben holding her, his relief wafting from his body into hers in waves, was doing something healing to her soul. It sewed a single stitch where she'd been ripped. A single stitch that put some of the gash back together and made all the difference. Slowly, she hugged him back.

No tears. He needs to see how strong you're getting.

"Get in the truck, so I can light into you properly. You scared the shit out of us. All of us."

"Where's the crew?" she asked, a little disappointed they weren't here to greet her so she could see them sooner.

"Greyson ordered them to stay home. He was afraid if you weren't okay..." Ben swallowed hard, his Adam's apple dipping into his muscular throat.

"What?"

A frown marred his features, and Ben wouldn't meet her eyes. Instead, he kicked at a pebble on the ground. "You feel different, Lynn. Not as sick, but..." He finally lifted those gold eyes to hers. "You're a dominant now, aren't you?"

"Not on purpose. It's just how the monster ended up. Now, what were you going to say? No sugar coating anything anymore. I want to know everything."

He bit the corner of his mouth and crossed his arms over his chest. With a resigned sigh, he admitted, "The crew isn't okay, Lynn. It's not like when you left. We thought we were gonna lose you, and it did bad things to everyone. There are holes in our bonds. Greyson took the crew just fine, but he was doing it while he was limping. You know? His first big act as alpha was going to be to put you down. He's not okay losing a crew member. None of us are. If you were as bad off as when you left? Greyson didn't want the crew to even see you. They would fold. Their animals are already seven shades of fucked up and unmanageable right now."

"But you're here."

"I asked to be the one to see you first. In case you asked me…"

"To put me down?"

Ben spat and gave her one jerky nod, and then was back to kicking the pebble with the toe of his work boot.

"I'm not asking for that anymore," she said, allowing steel into her voice. She leveled him with a look. "I'm fighting."

Ben rocked off from where he leaned on the front end of his truck and strode to the driver's side. "Good, because Beaston says war is coming, and no one in our crew is ready. You need to get them fighting, too." He yanked open his door and locked that intense gaze on her. "Time to do work, Lynn."

As he climbed into the cab of his truck, Lynn's phone dinged with a text message. Jathan's name popped up on the caller ID. The message was simple. It was perfect for this moment. He'd taken a picture of her brawling with Nox, son of the Cursed Bear. She looked like a fucking warrior, claws sunk in, teeth sunk in to his shoulder. Nox's huge, blond grizzly had his head thrown back in a roar of pain, and in the picture, her eyes were gold and focused right on the camera.

Be the badass, was all Jathan said.

A slow smile stretched Lynn's lips as Monster purred happily at his acceptance of both sides of her—flawed human and damaged animal.

Lynn made her way to the passenger's side of Ben's truck and climbed in.

Be the badass? Two weeks ago, it would've terrified Lynn to be that animal, but now Monster wasn't as scary.

Now she suspected Monster was part of the reason she was still standing.

SIXTEEN

"Whaaaat the fuck is going on?" Lynn murmured, leaning forward in the passenger's seat to better see the chaos out the front window of Ben's truck.

Jaxon's massive grizzly was fighting a panther and a lioness, Eden was sitting on top of Lynn's roof with her arms crossed over her legs, watching the fight with an empty gaze. Annalise, aka the host of a crazy panther named She-Devil, and Genevieve, Greyson's hearing-impaired mate, were grilling hot dogs like there wasn't a war kicking up plumes of dust right behind them.

Greyson was hitting golf balls into the woods with a nine iron, completely ignoring the fight, and Barret was lying on the ground in the middle of the clearing with a box of wine cradled in his arm, staring up at the sky like it was the most interesting thing he'd ever seen.

"This is the new normal," Ben said as he pulled into the clearing. "Welcome back to the C-Team."

The crew turned at once to the truck and tracked it with lightened eyes until Ben hit the brakes and eased to a stop. With a steadying breath, Lynn shoved open the door and slid out of the truck.

"Lynn?" Eden said from the roof. "Lynn?" she yelled louder as she jumped down, hitting the ground with almost zero impact to her legs before she was sprinting toward Lynn. There was her best friend. *Don't cry.* Lynn clamped her teeth down hard against her emotions, and was hit full on by Eden's hug. She lifted Lynn off the ground and carried her a few yards before she put her down again.

"Oh my God, oh my God," Eden repeated, easing back to cup her face, then hugging her again, cupping her face and hugging her. The others were rushing for Lynn now, which would've been fine, but Jaxon had pulled from his fight, and he didn't look too welcoming as he charged her. He looked pissed. He wasn't coming in for a hug like Eden. Clearly, Jax was out of control of his bear.

"Stop," Ben yelled, holding his hand out.

Greyson yelled louder, "Jaxon, stop!"

The enormous grizzly faltered but was still coming, and Monster screamed inside of her. That roar scratched up her throat as she turned to face the bruin. Jaxon's reaction to her roar was instant. He locked eyes with her as he slammed down against the ground and slid to a stop at her feet.

"Holy fuck," Greyson muttered as the others skidded to a stop before they reached Lynn. He twitched his startled golden gaze from Jaxon's frozen body to Lynn and back to Jax.

Barret was holding his box of wine to his chest like a shield. "Are you still Lynn?" he asked in a soft snarl.

She backed up a few paces and exposed her neck to her crew. "I'm Lynn. Just...different."

"Who did this to you?" Greyson asked.

She offered him a slow smile. "I'm doing it to me."

Barret shoved his box of wine into Annalise's arms and strode directly to Lynn, then smushed her against his chest.

"Stop," she said. "I have something to say to you."

Barret squeezed harder.

Lynn struggled out of his arms. The bad cat looked hurt. Pain swirled in his green eye while he ran his hand over and over his cropped hair.

"Barret?"

"Yeah?" he asked softly, ducking his gaze.

"Barret, I'm sorry."

His startled gaze lifted to her. "For what?"

"For dragging you into that fight with the lions. It was awful of me. I'm supposed to protect you because you're my crew. My people." Fuck, she was gonna cry. *Don't cry.* Lynn clenched her hands and swallowed hard to buy herself some time. "And I messed up. I wasn't thinking straight, and I was a coward. I didn't want to do that fight alone, and I could've gotten you killed."

He nodded for a long time, just…stared at her, bobbing his head, with a frown marring his eyebrows. "Can I hug you now?" he asked at last.

"You forgive me?"

"I forgave you for everything the night it happened, you emotional little man-eater, you. I knew you weren't in your right mind. Red, I never blamed you."

Stunned that he still cared enough to use his old nickname for her, Lynn stepped forward and slid her arms around his waist. Barret hugged the breath out of her, but breathing seemed really unimportant right now when the man she'd hurt was purring—*purring*—against her.

He rubbed his unshaven cheeks against one side of her head, and then the other, in a sign of affection.

With a helpless sound, Lynn melted against him. A hand rubbed her back, another gripped her arm, and another scratched the back of her head as she finally gave in and cried. The sunlight disappeared, and when she opened her eyes, they were all there, her crew, hugging her, wrapped around her like a blanket, these people who had *refused* to give up on her, even when she had given up on herself. There were more than a few sniffles, and it wasn't just from the girls. No one talked. They just touched. Touch was important for shifters, especially big cats. Time and time again, hands brushed her back, her head, her arms, as if they were reassuring themselves she was still here, still warm, and still breathing.

"The wieners are burning!" Kaylee, Anson's mate, suddenly shrieked.

Barret grabbed his dick. "My wiener's not

burning!"

Jaxon was butt-ass naked from his Change, and also covering his nethers as he watched Annalise sprint toward the grill. "Dude, she meant the hot dogs are burning," he muttered, reaching over with his free hand to slap Barret upside the head.

Barret punched Jax in the throat, and then they were wrestling on the ground, grunting and cussing at each other.

"No, stop," Anson deadpanned softly. "You'll hurt each other again."

Lynn observed the dark circles and the hollow faces of her crew. "Everyone looks like crap."

Half of Red Havoc had joined after she'd become two bubbles shy of an aquarium, so she didn't know the females that well other than Eden, and Genevieve, who had grown up near Damon's Mountains too. Annalise had automatically sprinted after Kaylee to help with the burning food though, and Eden was doing the same. Clearly there were bonds that had formed in the crew that she'd missed while she was on the crazy train. She had some catching up to do.

"Come on," Greyson, the new alpha of Red Havoc, said, slinging his arm over Lynn's shoulder. "You're probably tired. I'll get you settled in your tree house."

She parted her lips to respond, but her phone dinged with another text message. It was Jathan again, this time with a picture of her fighting Tagan, the alpha of the Ashe Crew. In it, Monster was crouched down, lips curled back in a hiss as she locked gazes with the snarling, giant grizzly. She wasn't backing down an inch.

Be the badass.

Lynn smiled and typed back, *I kind of love you, you know.*

I know. I miss you. Send me a picture of your tits tonight.

Lynn snorted and shoved her phone in her back pocket, then narrowed her eyes at her old house, the one she'd shared with Brody. The break in her heart had started here. "I think I need to stop living in treehouses. I came home, Greyson. I want to come all the way home."

He smiled at her proudly, then nodded. "I'll get your bag." He pulled her against his side in a hug before he made his way to Ben's truck, leaving Lynn to look after the crew who had gathered around the burnt food and were a mess of chaos. Almost all of them were arguing. Barret and Jax had stood up from wrestling and were jogging over to the food, but they were still kicking at each other every few steps like overgrown man-children. And when she caught Eden's eye, her friend smiled with a mushy look on her face. Eden was an albino falcon shifter with platinum blond hair and lightened eyes. She looked so relieved in this moment that it took Lynn's breath away.

This crew was a mess. They looked like they'd been dragged through Hell, and Lynn knew she was part of the reason they had been hurting. She loved them. She needed them.

Someday, she was going to make this Amberlynn's crew, and these complaining, neurotic, half-crazed, fun-loving, joy-making weirdos would be a part of her daughter's bigger family. And if she was really lucky and worked hard enough, perhaps Jathan would make a home here with her too.

Lynn owed it to everyone to fix what had been broken. And that started with banishing the ghosts from her old home and making it hers again.

Blink. Time was lost.

"Lynn!" Barret called from a table where he was squirting a ridiculous amount of mustard over about seventeen hotdogs he'd lined up. "Do you want six hotdogs or ten?"

Lynn shook her head, confused. She'd disappeared again, but it wasn't any darker, and no one had seemed to notice. And when she looked over at Ben's truck, Greyson was still pulling her bag out of it.

She'd disappeared, but only for a second.

Huh.

She texted Jathan. *I'm still with you.*

Did you disappear?

For just a second.

There was a long pause, and she felt that weight settling over her chest again, the one that shackled her to the ground when she disappointed people. But then right as she went to put her phone in her pocket, Jathan responded. *That's progress.*

And then there was a picture of her fighting Clinton in a weed-riddled yard covered in yellow dandelion flowers. Her coat was silky and black, a stark contrast to his coarse, blond fur. This picture was of her in mid-air, leaping for the Cursed Bear, front claws out, teeth bared, eyes on his throat. Beaston had told her, "Be the ripper."

Jathan texted, *Be the badass.*

Lynn walked deliberately to her old cabin, determined to be the tough girl everyone thought her to be.

Blink.

No. Stay here and deal. See it and then it won't be so hard.

Blink.

Please Monster. Wait.

Shadows took the corners of her vision, but determined, she jogged up the stairs and pushed the door open. Inside it was dark, so she flipped the light switch. There was a healthy layer of dust on everything, and the roof had leaked while she was away, causing water damage to the floor. But other than that, everything was just as she remembered. The walls were still the soft purple she'd painted them. It drew a tiny smile from her lips at the memory of how angry Ben had been for 'ruining the integrity of the log cabin.' She'd thrown out the old pictures of her and Brody the night she'd found his text messages to Winter. A white vase of dried, dead, disintegrating flowers sat on the table. Okay. She was doing pretty good with this. The edges of her vision were clearing, but she hadn't jumped the hardest hurdle in this home yet. With a determined march, Lynn strode to the back bedroom, the tiniest one, shoved the door open, and froze.

She'd decorated Amberlynn's nursery in baby ducks.

Blink.

No, no, no. Look, Monster. We were excited once. We had fun painting this room. We were going to be good at this.

She *was* going to be good at this.

Forcing her feet to move, Lynn made her way through the nursery, tidying the toys and books that she had read to her growing stomach when she was pregnant and all alone. All. Alone. She'd been surrounded by the crew, but had felt a world apart.

"Red, where the fuck are you?" Barret called through the house. "Ooooh," he murmured, easing into the doorway of the nursery and looking around. He balanced the giant platter of hot dogs in one hand and put his fingers to his lips, and without a single warning, the idiot blew the loudest, shrillest whistle imaginable and nearly ruptured her eardrums before she could cover her ears!

"Crew! Lynn's place looks like shit, and she needs us to seven dwarves her."

"What?"

"Like the movie where the dwarves clean up the house."

"Are you talking about Snow White? The dwarves messed up the house. The animals cleaned it."

"Great. I'm an animal, you're an animal. Jaxon's a chode hair, Anson's a smelly pile of bat guano, Annalise is okay when she's human, Kaylee ate all my fucking yogurt last Tuesday—"

"Oh my gosh, are we going to go through the entire crew?" Lynn asked impatiently.

"Well, I waaaas," Barret groused, cradling his platter of mustard-slathered wieners and buns.

"I'm gonna eat one of those," Lynn said, grabbing the one on the end.

"I made you a dozen," Barret said, frowning down at his double layer of dogs.

Lynn snorted. "You think I can eat a dozen?"

"Remember? We had a contest, and you ate a dozen. I ate like twenty-six and made fun of you because you were a pussy. And you said it wasn't fair because you weren't wearing the right pants."

"Oh yeaaah." Now it was coming back to her. That was before she was pregnant, before everything got messed up with Brody. She used to have fun. "I wasn't wearing my eating pants."

"Which is just yoga pants, let's be honest."

"You were wearing... Barret, now I remember, you were wearing a pair of *my* yoga pants." She giggled. "You stole them from my house, and they were those pink and black leopard print ones, and everyone could see the perfect outline of your dick and balls. It was so weird I told you to take them off because you were going to rip them, and you did rip them! When you bent over after you ate all those hotdogs, the crack ripped, and you weren't wearing underwear. You traumatized the entire crew." She barely got through the last part because she was laughing so much at the memory. Anson had barfed in the bushes in front of her house immediately following the *riiiiiip*.

"You remember how it was back then?" Barret asked, the smile fading from his lips.

She didn't remember a lot of it, so she just nodded so he wouldn't hear the lie in her voice. Her mind didn't work as well as it used to.

"You were happy, Lynn. We had fun. Sure, we were a crew of fuck-ups, and still are, but back before you hadn't let Brody control you yet, you smiled all the time. I watched when he started paying attention to you. You were lit up for a month, and then slowly, you started fading away. I watched the light die from your eyes, and I asked you over and over again if you were happy. Remember? And you would say yes, but your voice was hollow."

"You used to fight him all the time," she

murmured, a hundred battles between the two flashing across her mind like lightning strikes.

"Because I wanted to kill him. Ben kept stopping me. Sometimes it takes one bad apple to ruin a crew, Lynn. That bad apple? It was never you. Stop." He jammed a finger at her face where her eyes were burning. "Don't you fucking cry for him anymore. I'm glad he's dead, and you should be, too. You don't want no daddy like him for your cub."

"I want Jathan Barns," she whispered and pulled the neck of her shirt to the side.

Barret's green eyes flicked to the claiming mark on her shoulder. She would've laughed at his comically blank face if this was funny in any way.

"You're claimed, Red?"

She nodded.

The slow smile that stretched Barret's face was nothing short of wicked. "Greyson's gonna shit his pants. Are you bringing in another Gray Back? You're drawing the Bad Bear to Red Havoc

Territory? Both Barns twins in a panther crew?"

Another nod.

Barret tossed his head back and gave a booming laugh. "We're gonna have so many fights. Geez, Red! We're gonna bleed so much!" Another explosive laugh, and then he shoved a hotdog in his mouth. Around the bite, he said, "This if so fucking awefome. Everyone if gonna freak out. I'm telling Greyfon." He turned for the door. "Greyfon!!"

There was noise out in the front room. Lynn followed Barret out to find the crew cleaning dust off everything. Her cabin was small, and now extremely crowded with giant shifter bodies, but where she would've been instantly claustrophobic before when she was broken, now she leaned against the wall and watched the organized chaos with a strange, warm, tingling sensation thrumming through her torso. She was happy. She belonged. Anson leaned over and kissed his mate, Kaylee, in the kitchen. It was sweet, just a light kiss where their lips held, and then he leaned in and whispered something against her ear, drawing a giggle from her. It was such a tender moment, but it drew the smile off Lynn's face. She missed Jathan so badly it nearly doubled her over. She'd been tough all day, but watching them have an intimate moment made her want a hug from Jathan. Or a light touch on her back, a hand-hold, anything. There was such an acute pain in her chest, she had to fight to stay upright.

"What's wrong?" Eden asked as she settled against the wall beside her, flicking her platinum locks out of her face.

"I miss someone."

"I know."

Lynn frowned at her friend. "You do?"

"Last week, I called Jathan. We were all calling him," Eden explained with a giggle. "Red Havoc was relentless because we wanted to know everything that was happening with you. For the first few weeks, he was pissed. He would send us pictures of you fighting the shifters in

Damon's Mountains. He sent me a picture of you fighting my dad."

"Geez, I forgot Monster called Kellen to fight me. It's a little bit of a blur before last week."

Eden leaned her head on Lynn's shoulder. "Jathan was so upset, and we didn't understand why. He stopped answering our calls completely for a week, and then when I called this week, I expected his voicemail as usual. But he picked up. And his tone had changed. He told me, 'Eden, I didn't understand why you sent her here. I thought she was too far gone and I didn't understand why you were pushing her if she was dead already.' And then there was this big pause when I was thinking, *what the fuck is going on*? And then he said, 'She's really special. Now I understand. I'm gonna bring her back.' It was a promise. I've known Jathan my whole life, and he's never been serious about anything. He's never attached to anyone but Jaxon. After he hung up, I just sat there on the steps of your porch, with this gut feeling that he was going to follow through because I heard the honesty in his voice. And it wasn't just a challenge for him. Lynn, he said it like he loved you already. And ever since, I've been praying—*praying*—that you push Brody's memory to the side enough to let Jathan in. And just a few minutes ago, he called me. He told me if you ask for space to become stronger, to make sure the crew gives it to you, no questions asked."

Lynn rested her cheek on the top of Eden's hair. "That was really sweet of him to do."

"Well...he followed it with 'Remind Lynn to take pictures of her tits for me tonight,' so not that sweet, but I got the gist. He's special to you."

"He's very important to my story. He's maybe the reason I'm still here."

There was a long silence as they watched the crew cleaning dust from Lynn's house. At last, Eden murmured, "If he's the reason you're fighting again, then he's very important to me too."

****

Lynn locked her arms against the bathroom sink and stared at herself in the mirror. She hadn't really looked at herself much in the last year. Every time she did, she would see how far she had fallen. She had watched her eyes go vacant, her hair go limp, and the circles under her eyes darken. She'd lost weight, and her skin had turned pale. Her freckles, which had been light before, had made a stark contrast against her pallid skin. But today, she looked a little less like a ghost and a little more like her old self. Her red hair was healthy and shiny, hanging in waves down her shoulders. Her eyes were the soft brown of her human form, not the constant gold of Monster. She had color in her cheeks, and when she did a test smile, her eyes crinkled and danced. They weren't vacant anymore. She was really here. Really present.

"I brought girly booze," Anson announced.

Lynn jumped because she'd thought she was alone in the cabin. "Dude, you could knock!"

"Uh, I never knock, and where the fuck are

your pants?" Anson asked.

Lynn looked down at the extra-large T-shirt she'd stolen from Jathan right before she left. It smelled like him, and she wanted to sleep in it. Ignoring Anson's question, she asked, "What is girly booze?"

He stood there with two brown paper bags of clinking bottles while the other crew members trickled into her bedroom one by one.

Anson frowned down at his liquor store wares. "I got peach schnapps, vodka flavored with lime, watermelon, and raspberry, margarita mix someone had the audacity to put pink coloring in, tequila, orange juice, seven packages of fruit candy, and purple sugar granules for the rim of glasses, and a bunch of other stuff. I Googled the shit out of 'things girls like to drink,' because we're getting wasted tonight, and I'm one hundred percent tired of the girls complaining about only ever having beer here."

Eden grabbed one of the bags out of Anson's hands and looked into it with a beatific smile, like rays of heaven were coming out of the bag. "I'll be bartender!"

"No!" Barret yelled way too loud as he followed Eden out of the bedroom. "You make the weakest drinks. It'll take us a month to get drunk. I can get us drunk in eight ounces."

"That sounds disgusting," Annalise muttered, following the other two. "I'll help Eden."

"If we're doing this, we need glasses," Kaylee said.

Anson pulled pink and purple plastic cups from the other bag with a grin. "Y'all owe me a damn trophy. I'm MVP of Red Havoc tonight."

"False! I am," Barret called. "I pissed in your landscaping for the last week, and you didn't even notice."

"How does that make you MVP?" Anson asked, his voice fading as he left her bedroom. "And why the fuck would you do that?"

"Because I hate you. Where's the fruit candy?"

Greyson and Ben were the only ones who

remained, and both were leaning against the wall across the room, watching her with matching smiles.

"Hi, alphas," she said, crossing her arms and resting against the bathroom doorframe.

"Aw, I'm no alpha anymore," Ben murmured. He twitched his head toward the blond, tatted-up giant beside him. "That's Grey's burden now. I'm barely Second in the crew, and I'm pretty sure that's just because She-Devil lets me be. She half-assed bleeding me when I Challenged her for Second a couple weeks back."

"Where's Jenny?" Lynn asked. This part had troubled her. Ben's mate had been a pivotal part in the crew, but she was gone now, and there was a hole in this place.

"She's pregnant. Gonna give me another cub. She can't shift until the baby is born, and I can't have her here where she can't protect herself. She took the boys, Raif and Bentley, into hiding."

"Because of what Beaston says?"

Ben dipped his chin to his chest.

"Do you have a guess who is hunting us?"

It was Grey who spoke up. "Bentley is a Dunn lion cub. We know the Dunns will come for him at some point. That time might be now."

Lynn nearly choked on air. "Lions? Fuck. And I made it worse, pulling Barret into that fight with the Cold Mountain Pride."

Grey shrugged one shoulder up. "Bentley is safe. The cubs are safe, Jenny is safe, her unborn cub is safe, and Amberlynn is safest with your parents until this is done. The cubs...they're what matter. No more war-talk. You're finally home, and tonight we celebrate."

"With girly booze!" Anson called from the other room.

She shook off the nerves and giggled. "Okay, no more war-talk." She made her way past Grey and Ben, but hesitated at the door. "Grey?"

"Yeah?"

"Stay near me when the time comes, okay?"

His blond brows drew down slightly, but he nodded. "Okay. I'll protect you."

She smiled. There was no point in telling him he was going to be the one who needed protecting. She understood dominant males well enough that it would mind-fuck him before the fight. So she nodded and said, "I know you will," and made her way out to take a hideous pink shot Barret handed her. There was purple sugar and a pink Starburst candy on the rim of the pink plastic cup, but she took a picture because this made her happy, and she was determined to document her happiness for Jathan until they were together again.

Getting wild tonight, she messaged him, then attached the picture of her drink. Send.

Jathan responded almost instantly. *Thata girl. You were always wild. It's sexy as fuck. Take one for me tonight. I'm right here with you always.*

Lynn's cheeks heated with pleasure, and she read his text three times. She really loved him.

What are you doing? Send.

Barret interrupted her mushy musings, lifted his purple cup to Anson, and gave the worst toast ever. "To midnight landscape pee-pees. Oh, and the fish you found on your roof the other day was also me."

Anson shoved him in the shoulder, but drank anyway. So did the others. Lynn tossed hers back just as her phone dinged.

It was a picture. A selfie. In it there was a big, tattooed, burly, sexy man with dark eyes and dark hair. Her man. And in his arm was cradled a little red-headed baby who was fast asleep with her lips all puckered and her face smushed up in a sleep frown. One side of his body was in shadow as though he was sitting in a dark room, and the other was lit by the artificial light of a lamp. It took her breath away as her heart melted. Jathan's smile was just a slight curve, but there was adoration in it. This was beautiful to witness, her mate taking care of her child and bonding with her, even when Lynn wasn't there to ask him to do these things.

Oh, and also this... Jathan messaged. Next was a picture of him with a dead-eyed, unamused look, still cradling Amberlynn, but the camera was angled over his shoulder where Willa was standing there with her hands clasped in front of her mouth, staring down at the baby.

Ma won't leave me alone now. Get better fast so we can join you. They're gonna start calling me Crazy Jathan around here if I have to listen to all Ma's grandparent plans anymore.

Lynn responded with, *Oh my God, these are my favorite pictures ever and I'm going to frame them.*

Don't encourage her. Another image came through, and it was of Amberlynn sitting outside on a blanket surrounded by a tea party set. Fake butterflies hung on strands of fishing line from the tree she sat under. She was dressed as a worm.

Lynn gasped. *This is the cutestfuckingthing I've ever seen!*

Lynn, I miss you. I know why you have to do this on your own right now, but I really fucking miss you.

His seriousness drew her up short. It had never been like this with another man. Never before had anyone been able to get her heartbeat galloping with one sweet sentence. He actually wanted to be around her, like she wasn't a burden.

Jathan empowered her in ways she never thought a man could even do.

Miss you too. My chest hurts sometimes when I think about you. Send.

Not for long. That's just the bond digging at us for being apart. You've got this. You're doing so fucking good. I can tell. I'm really, really proud of you, Lynn. My mate is a monstah. I'm a lucky man.

He sent an image of her fighting the grizzly shifter, Bruiser, of the Ashe Crew.

Be the badass.

She huffed a laugh and shook her head. She really was a monstah, but Jathan seemed to like that about her, so okay. She was owning it.

That night, she drank with her crew. Too much perhaps, but it was fun, easy, and when they were tipsy and tired, they all sat on floors and chairs and couches in her living room and talked all night. She told them everything—what it was like when she was broken, what it was like when she disappeared, and she swallowed her fears and admitted all her sins and the guilt she'd carried that had gotten her to where she was in this moment. She told her crew everything, and somehow, someway, she felt lighter afterward. Jathan was already carrying the weight with her, and now her crew was too. Now they understood her better.

And in her heart, she knew things were going to be easier tomorrow because she didn't feel like an outsider anymore. She was Red Havoc through and through. She always had been, but things had gotten complicated the more she kept her pain to herself.

Not anymore.

With each regret she'd admitted out loud to her friends, another stitch had closed the wounds of her soul.

And when Grey twitched his head toward the front door and told her, "Time to Change on purpose," she only hesitated a moment.

Giving Monster her body after such progress was terrifying, but she needed to keep pushing her in the right direction, test her inner animal to gauge where her recovery was. Plus, Red Havoc was Changing with her. They were grizzlies, panthers, lions, and falcons, and Lynn wouldn't be alone with this Change. Not this time.

She followed her crew out the door, and when they had all Changed and were standing there under the full moonlight, waiting on her, she blinked on purpose. And time was lost, but only for a moment as her body changed to that of her panther. And then she was there, with Monster. She was actually present. She could see and feel and hear and control the animal's body, and she screamed out in triumph because it had been so long since she'd felt the breeze through her fur or heard the forest sounds with her sensitive ears.

After a few seconds, the roars and victorious cries of her crew lifted into the night air to answer her call.

And she was exactly as she was supposed to be.

SEVENTEEN

One week had been an eternity. She missed everything about Jathan, but she'd done it. She'd put in the work and bonded to her crew again. She was finding herself, both sides, Monster and Lynn, trying her best to make them more like one and less like two.

The crew had lifted her up when she needed it and given her space when she'd asked. Eden had bullied them into backing off any time she had said, "I need a minute."

Lynn held in a squeal of excitement as she connected the call. She leaned her back against the brick wall of Jessie's Brewskies where she'd excused herself from her shot-guzzling crew to call her mate. It was pouring down rain, and buckets of water were streaming from the awning she stood under, splashing to the ground and getting her flip-flops wet, but she didn't care. She bit her lip as the phone rang and rang again.

"Hey," Jathan greeted her in that deep, rumbling voice she'd spent hours every night talking too. "Tell me you have good news for me, woman. I'm dying here."

"You can't die. I need your dick."

He laughed and said, "Ask me then."

She made him wait a few seconds and tried to make her voice serious. "When I left Damon's Mountains—"

"Oh, my God, what's happening?" Jathan asked, panic in his voice. "Are you ending this?"

"Just kiddiiiiiing," she sang.

On a breath, Jathan muttered, "Oooh mother-fucking fuck you scared me. Don't do that. I already packed up my damn trailer and gave

Creed my notice."

Fighting back laughter, Lynn wrapped her free arm around her stomach and stomped on the ground in quick succession to get some of the excitement out. "Jathan Barns, will you move out here and make a life with me? Will you be part of my crew and have sex with me whenever I want and make me pizza rolls when I'm hungry and protect me from wasps because I super-hate wasps. And will you promise to stick with me even if I still disappear sometimes? And will you be good to me and Amberlynn when I get well enough to bring her home?" She sighed to expel some of the nerves. "Will you be a family with me?"

A few breaths went by before Jathan murmured in a soft, serious tone, "It's just..."

"Stop," she demanded through a nervous laugh.

"Lynn...I'm already here."

"What?"

"I've been here for two damn days, staying in

Saratoga because I couldn't keep away from you. I was fighting so hard to give you space to do what you needed on your own, but I've been in a motel here since Wednesday. I couldn't stand the thought of an upcoming war for your crew and me being so far away. I'm yours, little badass. I was just waiting on you to tell me you were ready. I was already your family. Amberlynn's, too. I have been since the day I bit you. I meant that claiming mark, Lynn. You girls have me."

Her stomach erupted in butterflies, and completely stunned, she stared at the cracks in the parking lot in front of her. "I don't have to wait to see you?"

"Nope. Give me five minutes to pack up at the hotel. I'm at a coffee shop right now, walkin' out to the truck."

"You didn't bring the Harley?"

"Of course I brought the Harley. I hauled that thing in a trailer with the rest of my belongings. I'm moving in, woman. Make me some room in your closet."

She belted out a laugh. "I'll give you three inches."

"I give you six inches," he said in a sultry voice. She could imagine him arching his eyebrow at her as he told that joke.

"Perv."

"You like it."

Genevieve opened the door to Jessie's and signed, *Are you okay?*

Lynn nodded and mouthed, *I'll be right in.*

"Uh, hold up on coming out here," she said to Jathan as she watched Gen duck back inside the bar. "We're in town."

"For what?"

"Beer?"

Jathan chuckled. "Is the crew partying tonight?"

"Um, you know how you said you wanted six dates?"

"Mmm hmmm," he drawled out.

"Well, would a night at Jesse's Brewskies with me and a crew of delinquent shifters count as a date?"

She could hear the smile in his voice when he said, "Hell yeah. I'll be there in a minute. I'll bring the truck so we can fuck."

Lynn cracked up, was smiling so big her face hurt. "So romantic and poetic."

"I'm only sweet and well-mannered for you. God, I can't wait to get both my hands on your ass. I wanna grab it so bad."

As much as his joking amused her, he was also turning her on right now. He'd revved her up for seven damn days with his nighttime dirty talks. "Touch you in a few minutes," she murmured cheekily.

"Fuck. Yes. I'm ready." The line went dead, and now the nervous flutters were warring with the butterflies.

She hadn't seen him in a few days, and she'd gone through a lot of changes since she'd been in Damon's Mountains. What if he didn't like the person she was becoming? What if who she was didn't work for him anymore?

Stop it. He likes strong women, he's been telling you to be the badass, he'll like you just fine. Probably.

She paced the sidewalk, stepping over dandelions that had stubbornly grown in the cracks, avoiding the spots where the rain was pouring over the side of the roof. She couldn't believe she got to see him so soon. She'd expected to have to wait a few days while he got things in order and traveled here, but there was zero wait time. But also zero time to prepare for his arrival. She probably would've worn something sexier than cut-off jean shorts and an old, threadbare Moosey's Bait and BBQ T-shirt she got when she was in high school. Her two-dollar flip-flops clacked with each step. He probably wouldn't care that she hadn't dressed up...right? Crap, why was she so nervous all the sudden? *Be the badass.* Oh God, there was his truck. Jacked up, black-on-black F-150 with a *Grizzly & Proud* sticker in the back window.

Her nerves disappeared the second he

parked, kicked open his door, and locked eyes on her. His whole face transformed into a grin as he dragged his hungry gaze down her body, pausing on her curves. He wore a black baseball cap and a black T-shirt that was tight on his torso and muscular arms, highlighting all those sexy tattoos. The rain made darker spots all over his shoulders as he stood there. He was as tall as his lifted truck and as wide as the broadside of a barn, with a thick muscular neck she wanted to bite for some reason she wasn't going to think about too much.

Lynn bolted for him and didn't slow at all as he jogged toward her. He leaned down slightly with his arms out and caught her full force against his chest. He grunted but didn't even stumble under her weight. Losing her mind, she wrapped her legs around his waist and laid kisses down his cheek to his neck where she clamped down her teeth as the rain poured on them.

"Gonna get yourself fucked right here if you

don't quit it, you bitey little thing," Jathan snarled.

He pulled the back of her hair, easing her off his throat, and then his lips crashed onto hers. Rough man gripped her hair even tighter and plunged his tongue into her mouth over and over, possessing her completely, owning her, dominating the kiss until nothing existed outside of where their bodies touched.

"I missed you, I missed you, I love you, I love you," she murmured mindlessly against his lips as she clung to his neck tightly.

His hands were rough in her hair and on her ass. She hoped he left a bruise back there. Her shifter healing was getting faster the stronger she got, but at least it might stay for an hour. She wanted to be marked by him. Wanted it rough right now.

With a low, rumbling snarl in his chest, Jathan spun them around and strode for his truck. "I can't wait. I was gonna try to, but I can't. I need to be inside you now. Right fuckin' now."

Yes, yes, yes to all of that. He yanked open the driver's side door of his truck, and she scrambled across the console to her seat. As soon as he was settled behind the wheel, she slid one hand up his shirt and the other into the waist of his jeans.

As her fingers brushed the swollen head of his cock, she gave a purr of relief. *Mine. All mine.*

The engine roared to life. Jathan wore a wicked grin on his face as he slid his hand behind her head and pulled her face gently toward his lap. Sexy Bad Bear.

As he hit the gas and drove the truck out of the parking lot, she unfastened his jeans and unsheathed him, then slid her lips over his hard cock. She'd almost forgotten how big he was. Jathan groaned and rocked his hips up as she took him. His hand was still in her hair, but he wasn't forcing her lower. When she took him in her mouth again, he rolled his hips to the pace she set. He muttered a cuss word, and the steering wheel creaked with the grip of his hand as he drove. Ooooh, she loved this kind of control.

She sped up her rhythm when he groaned again. His leg muscles twitched under her hand, and she gripped him at the base and sucked hard on him.

The truck rocked to a stop. He pulled her up and shoved his jeans down his thighs. "Ride me," he growled out, yanking the button on her shorts.

Oh, hell yes. It was dark where he'd parked, on the edge of some woods. On the right of the truck, there was a chain-link fence surrounding a small power plant in the middle of the woods. On the left, she could see Jessie's Brewskies through the trees. They were on some sort of gravel road. It was completely dark, and the moonlight peeking through the clouds in the distance cast everything in a blue hue.

Desperately, Lynn shoved out of her shorts and panties, kicked them off her ankles, and crawled over the console. Jathan gripped her hips and threw his head back against the seat when she slid over his cock. She was tight but wet enough to take him.

"Fuck, you feel so good," he groaned. He slid deeper into her and then with a hard grip on her hips, eased her up, then slammed her down again.

Lynn snarled and clenched the back of his dark hair, lifted her chin, and shook her head slowly. She wanted control tonight. A slow, feral smile took Jathan's lips, and his eyes blazed an inhuman green. Sexy, sexy, sexy man.

Lynn let him drive deep into her, but then stayed there, rocking gently, rocking slowly, torturing him as he gripped her ass. He was trying to let her keep control, she could tell, but every few strokes, he would let off an impatient growl and grit his teeth. Oh, he felt so good, bumping her clit with each rock of their hips, and now the pressure was building in her center. Wrapping her arms around his neck and smashing her chest to his, she sped up. She moaned at how good he felt that deep inside of her. Faster, faster they slammed against each other, and he was snarling constantly now. His lips would go to her neck, then her mouth, to her neck, to her mouth.

When his hand went up her shirt and slipped under her bra, she tossed her head back, his name riding her lips. Rough man, rough hands, calloused and strong from the work he did. So close.

"Louder," he gritted out. "Fucking scream it."

"Jathan!"

Orgasm exploded through her body, rocking her to the core as Jathan lurched against her. His thick shaft throbbed inside of her, over and over, matching her release and filling her with warmth. His arms shook as he held her tightly against him, bucking into her body, emptying himself completely. He slowed, smoothing out his rhythm, pulsing softly into her, pulling every last aftershock of her release from her. Good man, coveting her, even after he'd had his fill. His hands gentled on her ass, and eventually, they slid up her back. And when they stilled, melted against each other, completely spent, he just hugged her. He held her and pressed his lips gently to her cheek, nose, neck , ears and then her lips, as if he hadn't tasted her in years instead of just a week.

He eased back and searched her eyes. His face was cast in highlights and blue shadows from the moon hanging low in the sky behind her. As she ran her knuckles gently against his dark beard, he parted his lips to say something, but his attention flickered to something behind her. Jathan's entire body went rigid, and shock filled his blazing green eyes.

Chills rippled across her skin as she turned slowly to see what had him so enthralled. Through the drops of rain racing down the front window, twenty yards off, a silverback gorilla stalked slowly through the woods in the direction of Jessies Brewskies, eyes intent on the town lights through the trees. Behind him a female gorilla was walking on all fours in the same direction. And behind her? A fully mature male lion. And another. And another. The woods came alive with movement.

"What the fuck?" Lynn whispered on a horrified breath.

Jathan pulled the seat lever and yanked her down on top of him so fast she gasped. They lay flat in his truck, her face pressed against his neck, her body trembling in fear.

"They're going after Red Havoc," she breathed against his ear. "In public. Why?"

"Because then no one can help your crew." Jathan's voice was so soft it was barely a breeze against her eardrum. He was texting with one hand, the glow of the screen lighting up the interior of his truck. That glow was going to get them busted, but Jathan whispered, "I didn't come alone."

When Lynn looked at his phone, the person he was texting was listed as The Blue Dragon.

His grip tightened on her hair as something bumped the truck.

In a whisper, he said against her ear, "The shifters of Damon's Mountains can't help if this war is public. Everyone would recognize them."

Something bumped the truck harder.

Blink.

"Lynn, not yet. We have to get Red Havoc to the woods. Don't. Change. Yet."

Blink.

Jathan's grip tightened around her. "Wait."

The truck rocked up on two wheels and glass shattered inward with a deafening crash. A meaty hand gripped her arm, and Lynn screamed as she was yanked away from Jathan by a massive gorilla. Window glass cut her thigh as she was pulled through the opening, and the pain was instant. She was flying through the air, thrown by the silverback, and didn't even have enough time to call Monster. She was shocked. She was going to hit the fence and then the ground, but right before impact, a massive, tattooed arm snaked out and hooked her around the waist, cushioning her. She still fell, but it wasn't like it would've been.

Jathan was scary-fast and had gotten to her. He stood in front of her, facing off with three gorillas—the silverback and two females. Two lionesses were also slinking this way. They were two against an army of mixed shifters, who had clearly become allies against Red Havoc—lions and gorillas, warring together for the first time in shifter history.

Jathan looked like a damn beast in the moonlight, body tensed and puffed up, a snarl rattling from his chest as he eased her toward the fence.

"Lynn, don't Change until you get to the bar. You need to get Red Havoc to the woods so Damon can help them."

"What will you do?" Damn her voice as it shook like a dry leaf in autumn.

"I'm gonna buy you time."

"But there's too many," she whispered in terror.

He gave her a fiery glance over his shoulder.

"Get to Greyson. Run, Lynn." And then an enormous bruin grizzly exploded from his body with a force so big, she was thrown into the chain-link fence.

A snarl sounded behind her, and she turned just in time to see a lion running straight for her from the other side of the fence. With a shriek, she pushed off it, just as Jathan charged the silverbacks. The force of them hitting each other reverberated through her chest, and for one terror-filled moment, she watched the violence Jathan was capable of. He really was Monster, just like her. He ripped and shredded the gorillas with teeth and claws, and as much as she wanted to stay here and make sure he finished them, he'd asked her to run. To find Greyson.

She forced her legs to move, and in the woods near her, the two lionesses pulled their focus from Jathan's fight and arched it to her. Fuck, she was giving them a perfect target on her back as she ran.

Monster snarled inside of her.

"Not yet," she whispered, pushing her legs harder and harder. Jathan was right. If she Changed now, Monster would turn around and fight every last shifter coming for her. She wouldn't be able to tell the crew they could get help if they made it to the woods. She wouldn't be there for Grey and whatever was happening inside the bar right now.

Fuck! Dunn lions? Cold Mountain Pride? Gorillas? There were so many, all allied with the sole purpose of snuffing her crew from the history books. Red Havoc had made lethal enemies.

She could feel them behind her now, hear them growling and panting. The hairs lifted on her body. At the last second, she pulled off sharply to the right. One of the lionesses had been mid-leap and went flying into an oak, but one of them skidded through the dry leaves on the ground and kept coming.

Almost to the street!

Now! Monster growled louder inside of her.

Blink.

"Not yet!"

There was chaos in the parking lot of Jessie's, and smoke billowed from one side of the bar. Lion's and gorillas were everywhere, focused on something happening on the side of the building. A panther screamed. Fuck, that was Barret. Another screamed, and a bear roared. Jaxon. Behind her, another roar bellowed, answering his twin. Jathan.

Fury boiled in her blood, tinging her vision with red. *Blink.*

"Not. Yet."

She could see them now. There was a crowd around her crew, so many lions, so many gorillas. Humans were scattering in the parking lot and street like roaches running from the sunlight. The air was filled with screaming.

Now? For fuck's sake now, or we'll lose them!

"Not. Fucking. Yet," Lynn gritted out.

She shoved between two female gorillas who were set to pound their fists onto Jaxon's grizzly.

Lynn ducked under his belly just as he reared back and raked his powerful claw against the arm of one of the gorillas. The war had already started, and Red Havoc was locked in battle with every shifter that could reach them. Her crew was losing. Bleeding. Eden was swooping down and clawing at faces, trying to give them relief. Kaylee's lioness was brawling with two male lions, and She-Devil had gone straight murder-cat on two lionesses already, but had three more on her now. Greyson. Where the fuck was Greyson? There. He was off to the side. He'd been hunted and separated. He was clear on the other side of the parking lot, his panther brawling, but being dragged and herded by four gorillas.

"Get to the woods!" she screamed as a lioness closed in on her race toward Greyson. "We'll have help if we get to the woods!" God, let her crew have heard her desperate instruction. Let Greyson have heard her.

The lioness was on her.

Now? Monster screamed in her middle.

Lynn pumped her fists and zeroed in on the silverback about to batter Greyson with his fists.

"Now."

Blink. No time was lost.

Pain ripped through her as Monster took over her body. Black fur, lithe body, teeth and claws. She had weapons now. Weapons she was going to use to maim every fucking one of these assholes who were hurting her crew. Who were hurting Jathan.

She hit the ground on all fours and ducked the lioness, gave that bitch her back as she slammed into the silverback just as he was blasting his fists down on Greyson. Pain clawed down her side, and she sank her teeth into the gorilla's throat. The silverback gripped her neck and went to fling her away, but she'd hit his kill spot. He was already dead, and he didn't even know it. She pushed off him—ripping with her teeth. The ripper. She was the badass. There were so many she lost track. She sliced and clawed and bit and spun and attacked, kept those mother fuckers off her alpha as he waged war on so many. Soooo many. Grey was a war machine. She was a war machine. Eden was helping. She was dive-bombing the masses that kept coming. Through the haze, she could hear panther screams. They were closer to the woods, crossing the street and heading for the trees. They were calling her and Grey, but it was too hard to get away. Lynn and her alpha were being pushed toward the burning bar.

Grey was fighting two males now. She didn't recognize them, but they had to be Dunn lions. They were massive with black manes, a Dunn trait. A female gorilla rushed her, but Lynn's leg was stuck in the pile of bodies she'd tried to step over. Panicking, she pulled her leg, but it was stuck like cement. Shit! She hunched just as the gorilla came flying through the air, and time slowed. Lynn screamed, promising death if the gorilla touched her. Greyson's panther screamed in pain behind her. The gorilla was in the air, arms out, silver eyes intent on her, black lips pulled back, baring long canines that would puncture Lynn's body in a matter of moments.

And then something monstrous came out of the sky, straight down at them, with such power, Lynn was blasted backward, twisting her back leg painfully. All she saw were red belly scales as the wind from the dragon's wings flattened her against the concrete and stole the air from her lungs. His enormous claws raked the concrete beside Lynn and Greyson as he picked up the two Dunn lions and the gorilla in an instant. With a powerful beat of his wings, the red dragon, Vyr, son of Damon, arched his back and pushed off the ground, creating and earthquake as he aimed for the sky.

The silverback and the two Dunns were gone, and no fire filled the air above them, raining ashes and an arc of burning magma. Vyr wasn't minding Damon's rules to not be seen in a war. There would be video footage of this, but the red dragon apparently gave zero shits about that. And when Lynn eased her throbbing leg out from between the two lion bodies, she looked up to see Nox's blond grizzly and Torren's green-eyed silverback mauling a pair of gorilla shifters. If they didn't die in this battle, Damon Daye was going to filet them.

A firm swat on her rump pulled her attention to Greyson, who was urging her forward. Fire blasted down through the parking lot, lighting up cars and causing a new wave of screams from crowds of running humans. Vyr wasn't a careful dragon, and as important as it was to get to the woods to get help from ally shifters, it was equally important to get as far away from Vyr's fire as possible. He would char them alive and lose zero sleep over the mistake. That dragon was fucking *terrifying*.

Lynn bolted after Greyson as best as she could, ignoring the pain of her back leg and the claw marks that crisscrossed her body. How long had they been fighting? It felt like hours. She was exhausted, but fueled by adrenaline. How badly was Greyson hurt? He was running in front of her, not favoring injuries, but his coat was matted and he smelled of blood. A lot of blood. Too much. Fuck. She knew why he was important. The crew had almost folded losing her, and who was she? Bottom of the crew. If Red Havoc lost its alpha right now, right when it was crippled from losing Brody, and almost her, and with power shifting from Ben to Grey, they would all go crazy, just like her. It would be too much.

Greyson made it to the street, aiming for the woods beyond, but when he reached the solid white line, right in the center of the road, he was hit hard by a Dunn. There were so many enemy shifters cluttering the street and woods beyond. There had to be fifty lions and gorillas. Fifty against one crew. She hated them. *Hated* them.

Lynn leapt onto the lion's back and sank her teeth into his neck. His mane was thick, and made it harder to hurt him fatally. This lion was the biggest she'd ever seen. He was easily three times her size. Black Dunn mane, and he reeked of a dominance so potent she choked on it. Couldn't breathe! He had his teeth on Grey's neck though. Her alpha was brawling, but the Dunn lion had to be on his neck. A kill bite. Fuck, fuck, fuck, she needed to end this before the alpha of the Dunn's ended Greyson. He was pinned under the weight of the lion, and though he was clawing like some demon escaping hell and doing damage to the lion's stomach, ribs, and face, it wasn't enough.

"Be the ripper," Beaston demanded, his powerful voice echoing over the screams and chaos.

Beaston?

He stood at the edge of the woods, green eyes blazing, hands behind his back, chin held high. "You are exactly as you're supposed to be."

She needed to be Lynn, but she also needed to be Monster.

In desperation, she blinked.

And time was lost.

EIGHTEEN

Jathan saw her. She was running after Grey, covering her alpha as he tried to get to the woods. She'd made it to him, told him what he needed to do, and now she was protecting his weak side.

Grey was hurt. It was bad. Jathan could see the Dunn alpha coming for him, right in the middle of the street, but he couldn't get to them fast enough. He charged from the forest, desperate to reach the two panthers, but just as the Dunn alpha had slammed into Grey, Beaston stood in front of him, appearing out of nowhere like a ghost, hands out. He didn't say anything, just stood there, blocking Jathan.

Behind him, the woods came alive. The trees came alive with snowy owls, falcons, and ravens. Bears, tigers, gorillas, and boars stepped out of the shadows, and the chaos died down around them. Above, the wind was a hurricane with the beating of dragons' wings. Not just Vyr either. The blue dragon was in the sky, ready to rain hell down on the Dunns and the gorillas. Damon was here, out in the open. More circled, blocking out the clouds. Dark Kane, the monstrous black dragon, the End of Days was here, which meant his Blackwing crew was in the woods behind them. Two smaller green dragons flew together, one right above the other—Diem and her daughter, Harper, alpha of the Bloodrunner Crew. Holy shit. Damon and Beaston had gathered everyone, just in case.

The second Lynn leapt onto the back of that massive Dunn alpha, all Jathan wanted to do was protect her. But Beaston had given him a warning look and turned to Lynn. He called out for her to be the ripper. He told her she was exactly as she was supposed to be.

Her eyes had trained on Beaston, and then a moment later, they'd gone dead. Lynn had disappeared. In her place, only Monster remained. And even Jathan winced as she clamped down and bit through the spine of the Dunn alpha. The beast jerked under her, then released Grey's neck and slumped over.

Monster didn't let go. She crouched defensively by her kill.

Jathan tucked his bear back into his body and gasped at the pain of the claw marks that covered him. He was exhausted, barely able to stand, but he stumbled to her. Rain pouring down from the storm clouds above, he stood there watching the shifter he loved fulfill what she was born to do.

Genevieve, Greyson's mate, was human again, yelling in a voice too loud because she was deaf and couldn't hear herself. She was pressing her hands against her mate's throat as he lay there in the street. Tendrils of red streamed slowly away from his body, mixing with the rainwater. He panted, his throat gurgling, and Gen was crying, sobbing, begging help. Jathan stepped forward to assist, but Annalise was suddenly there, and Kaylee. Jathan was numb. He couldn't understand the words they were yelling as the Red Havoc Crew surrounded their alpha, trying to save him. All but Lynn, who stared vacantly at Jathan, her teeth clamped onto the lion's neck, her face buried in his thick mane. Her gold eyes were like Vyr's fire, daring him to take her kill.

Such a feeling of déjà vu hit him as he looked down at his ruined torso to the pink that streamed down his wet body. This was exactly as Beaston had described in his vision.

Around them, the remaining Dunns and gorillas were fleeing. Probably thanks to all the shifters from Damon's Mountains, Harper's Mountains, and Kane's Mountains melting out of the woods. On the other side of the street, a few brave humans remained, phones pointed at them, taking video. The fallout from this would be awful, but he couldn't worry about that now. They would have to face that hurdle when they got to it.

Right now, all he cared about was getting Lynn back.

He knelt in front of her and whispered, "Medusa."

Nothing. Still, she stared vacantly back.

"Can you hear me?"

Nothing.

Swallowing hard, he whispered, "Lynn, you did it. You became the badass." He smiled proudly at her. "I love you."

She blinked slowly, and her pupils constricted, focusing on him. In an instant, she released the lion, looking startled. Crouching on her belly, she backed off a few quick steps and looked around. Her gaze paused on the burning bar, on the demolished cars in the parking lot. On the scorched earth, and the humans across the street with their camera phones pointed at her. On the woods with all the shifters staring back at her. To the dragons in the sky. Beaston. Her crew working on Greyson. And finally back to Jathan.

Slowly, painfully slowly, she tucked Monster away, and then, naked and bleeding from the claw marks, she sat there on her folded knees. Her red hair was plastered to her face, and her eyes were still gold with tiny pupils. She snarled up her lip, his badass, and then she said in a hoarse voice, "Is it over?"

"The crew of two wars is the crew of two wars won," Beaston said. "It's over."

Lynn deflated, as though completely drained, and Jathan rushed to catch her before she hit the pavement. He hugged her close to his body and wished to God he could take her pain into him.

"Jathan?" she murmured, eyes on her crew working frantically on Greyson. "If Grey doesn't make it—"

"He will."

"If he doesn't, we won't be okay."

Jathan leaned down and kissed her gently. "Do you trust me?"

She nodded, eyes full of emotion as she opened them.

"Everything will be okay. Are you still here with me?"

Lynn blinked slowly but opened her eyes and focused on him again. With the tiniest smile pulling at the corner of her lips, she whispered, "Yeah, I'm still here."

EPILOGUE

Three months.

Three months since she'd left Damon's Mountains determined to get stronger.

Three months since the second war.

Three months since humans had uploaded shaky video of the shifters destroying Covington.

Three months since the government had opened an official investigation into who was to blame for all the casualties and all the damage to the town.

Three months since Red Havoc thought they were going to lose their alpha.

Greyson was watching her. He did that a lot. Ghost cat, always worried she would backslide, but she would prove herself to him, and to the rest of Red Havoc, with time. She smiled at him where he sat balanced on the back two legs of his neon blue, plastic chair. Grey had his hands linked behind his head, and when he was busted watching her, he smiled unapologetically. His neck was so scarred up now, not even his tattoos could hide the damage, but he didn't seem to mind.

This life required scars, Lynn had come to learn. Some were on the outside, and some they carried on the inside. But scars weren't shameful. They meant survival. They meant putting in work. They meant sticking around and getting through the hard stuff just on the chance that things could get better.

And for Lynn, things *had* gotten better— better than she'd ever imagined.

"All I'm saying," Jaxon said, "is that I feel sorry for you, Lynn."

She snorted and rolled her eyes. "I don't even want to know," she said, nestling closer to Jathan in his lap. He'd been scratching her back for the last half an hour, calming her, but he was as quiet as she was because they were waiting for something important.

"You picked the twin who got the genetic deficit for dick size."

"Oh my God," Annalise complained from where she stood by the grill, flipping steaks and corn on the cob. "Again? We have to talk about your dicks again?"

"Always!" Jax said. "We always have to talk about them because that shithead won't stop burning the words *my dick is way bigger* into our front yard! Four weeks in a row? Really?"

"That wasn't me, bro," Jathan said in a bored voice.

"Screw you, yes it was," Jax scoffed. "You used to do the same thing when we lived with the Gray backs. Clinton taught me how to do that too, just so you know. Next week I'm burning a life-sized portrait of my dick into your stupid yard. It's gonna be enormous."

Nearly unseating Lynn off his lap, Jathan leaned over and kicked the leg of Jaxon's chair so hard, he fell backward, yelling a string of curses that would make a sailor blush.

"Language!" Jenny, Ben's mate, admonished, jamming her finger at the two six-year-old panther and lion cubs playing near the entrance of the clearing. "The last thing I need is the boys repeating 'suck my hairy balls' at school. They already get in trouble enough with what Barret's been teaching them."

"I simply taught them how to grow plants," Barret defended himself from where he was sitting behind Eden.

Weed, Genevieve signed. *You taught them how to grow weed.*

"One of these days, Barret..." Jenny's warning tapered off as she stared up at the sky through her oversize red sunglasses. She rubbed the swell of her belly. She was tanning on a plastic recliner in a red and white polka-dot bikini.

Barret paused from his diligent work of making a hundred tiny little braids in Eden's blond hair to scoff, "One of these days, what?"

"I'm gonna kick you in your hairy balls," Jenny muttered. Ben bellowed a single laugh from where he was putting fresh logs in the fire pit for the next crew bonfire.

As Barret tied a little pink rubber band into the braid he'd just finished in Eden's hair, he griped primly, "I'm tired of everyone always picking on me."

Anson rubbed his eyes and made crying noises.

"Shut up, Anson! I get in trouble all the time, and I don't even do anything wrong."

"Oh yeah?" Kaylee asked from where she was lounging in Anson's lap. "Who really burned the words *my dick is way bigger* into Jax and Annalise's yard? Hmm?"

"It's not wrong if it's true," Barret barked out remorselessly.

Jax hadn't bothered getting up yet from where he'd fallen and lifted his head off the ground high enough to glare at Barret. "Are you fuckin' kidding me? *You* did it?" He picked up an empty blue beer can beside him and chucked it at Barret, who was flipping Kaylee off. The tin bounced off his forehead with a hollow *thunk*, and now Lynn was laughing right along with the others.

God, this crew was a mess. She loved them.

The sound of a car engine rumbled through the clearing, and Raif and Bentley stopped playing in the mud in the dirt road. "Mom! They're here!" Bentley yelled as the two boys stood and sprinted back toward them.

Lynn's heart began drumming against her chest. She looked over her shoulder at Jathan, but he was smiling so big she couldn't be nervous if she tried.

"Are you ready?" he asked.

Three months ago, she'd told her parents she wasn't ready to keep Amberlynn safe yet. There had been too much work to do on herself before she knew she could give her the life she deserved. Today things were different because she'd patched up her inside scars and done the work. Her eyes prickled with emotion, and she nodded. "I'm ready. Jathan?"

"Yeah?" he asked, brushing his knuckle down her cheek.

"I'll be good at this, right?"

"You're gonna be amazing. And I'm gonna be right here with you." There were honest tones infused in every word, so she had to believe him, because he truly believed in her.

Her dad's old Pontiac bounced and bumped up the gravel road, and Lynn stood. Behind her Jathan hugged his arms around her chest and pressed a comforting kiss against her temple.

Everything was prepared. Amberlynn's nursery was ready for her to sleep there. Lynn had bought everything she needed for her baby to come home. She'd felt this huge hole and massive weight in the last few months that she hadn't understood until right now, this moment.

The last puzzle piece that had been missing from her life was sitting in a little car seat in that black Pontiac.

The crew touched her as she walked past them, just a brush of fingertips against her arms that warmed her from the inside out. Jathan gripped her hand in his massive one. So strong and safe. He'd been her safe place from the second she'd left here for Damon's Mountains. He'd been the one to take her away from here, the one to begin fixing her insides, and the one to send her home. In this moment, holding his hand, feeling the soft touches from her crew as she made her way toward the car—toward a happy future—she felt like the luckiest person in the world.

When Mom got out, she was already crying. This had to be hard on them, giving up the child they'd raised for the last year, but when Lynn opened her mouth to apologize, Mom hugged her up tight and whispered in her ear, "I'm so proud of you."

Lynn hugged her back, gripping her shirt. It felt so damn good to make people proud instead of disappointed. And then Dad was there, and she could tell he was proud too, just from his smile. "It's so damn good to see you like this, Lynn. This is where me and your mom always dreamed of you ending up."

"In Red Havoc?" she asked, her eyes glued to the gurgling little redhead in his arm.

"No, baby girl. Happy. You look so happy. I can feel it coming off you in waves."

Dad handed her Amberlynn, and Lynn did her best not to fall apart as she brought her to her hip and rested her forehead on her daughter's. Beside her, Dad shook Jathan's hand in that mannish way big dominant male shifters did.

"Hi, baby," she whispered, rocking back and forth.

Amberlynn began playing with a lock of Lynn's hair. It was such a simple thing to happen, but something she thought she'd never get to be a part of. She'd been so close to gone, and now here she was, in this moment, with her crew and her parents. With her mate and her daughter. Her daughter.

Jathan's hand was rubbing her back now, and she looked up at him through her tears. His dark eyes were full, too. He scrubbed his hand down his beard, then leaned down and cupped the back of Amberlynn's head. He kissed the top of it, and then he did the same to Lynn, but stayed there, hugging her close. "My girls," he said in a thick voice.

It was the best feeling in the world to go from complete numbness to holding her little girl in her arms, having her heart so full. She was overwhelmed with joy as she stood there, holding her baby, surrounded by Jathan's strength. Moments like these were what made a lifetime. They were what made a life great. Her life was *amazing*, and she was so glad she hadn't quit.

Now...

Lynn was a survivor.

She was a fighter.

She was a proud Red Havoc panther.

A friend.

A daughter.

A *mate*.

She was a *mother*.

She was exactly as she was supposed to be.

~~The End~~

The Beginning

Want more of these characters?

Red Havoc Bad Bear is the fifth book in the Red Havoc Panthers series.

For more of these characters, check out these other books from T. S. Joyce.

Red Havoc Rogue
(Red Havoc Panthers, Book 1)

Red Havoc Rebel
(Red Havoc Panthers, Book 2)

Red Havoc Bad Cat
(Red Havoc Panthers, Book 3)

Red Havoc Guardian
(Red Havoc Panthers, Book 4)

This is a spinoff series set in the Damon's Mountains universe. Start with Lumberjack Werebear to enjoy the very beginning of this adventure.

About the Author

T.S. Joyce is devoted to bringing hot shifter romances to readers. Hungry alpha males are her calling card, and the wilder the men, the more she'll make them pour their hearts out. She werebear swears there'll be no swooning heroines in her books. It takes tough-as-nails women to handle her shifters.

She lives in a tiny town, outside of a tiny city, and devotes her life to writing big stories. Foodie, wolf whisperer, ninja, thief of tiny bottles of awesome smelling hotel shampoo, nap connoisseur, movie fanatic, and zombie slayer, and most of this bio is true.

Bear Shifters? Check

Smoldering Alpha Hotness? Double Check

Sexy Scenes? Fasten up your girdles, ladies and gents, it's gonna to be a wild ride.

For more information on T. S. Joyce's work,
visit her website at
www.tsjoyce.com

Made in the USA
Lexington, KY
02 February 2018